THAT TIME IN PARIS

A WOLFGANG PIERCE THRILLER

LOGAN RYLES

Copyright © 2021 by Logan Ryles. All rights reserved.

No part of this book may be reproduced in any form or by any electronic or mechanical means, including information storage and retrieval systems, without written permission from the publisher, except for the use of brief quotations in a book review.

THAT TIME IN PARIS is a work of fiction. Names, characters, places, and incidents either are the product of the author's imagination or are used fictitiously. Any resemblance to actual persons, living or dead, events, or locales is entirely coincidental.

ISBN: 978-1-7359031-2-5

Library of Congress Control Number: 2021911722

Published by Ryker Morgan Publishing.

ALSO BY LOGAN RYLES

THE WOLFGANG PIERCE SERIES

Prequel: *That Time in Appalachia* (read for free at LoganRyles.com)

Book 1: *That Time in Paris*

Book 2: *That Time in Cairo*

Book 3: *That Time in Moscow*

Book 4: *That Time in Rio*

Book 5: *That Time in Tokyo*

Book 6: *That Time in Sydney*

THE REED MONTGOMERY SERIES

Prequel: *Sandbox*, a short story (read for free at LoganRyles.com)

Book 1: *Overwatch*

Book 2: *Hunt to Kill*

Book 3: *Total War*

Book 4: *Smoke and Mirrors*

Book 5: *Survivor*

Book 6: *Death Cycle*

Book 7: *Sundown*

THE PROSECUTION FORCE SERIES

Book 1: *Brink of War*
Book 2: *First Strike*
Book 3: *Election Day*

For Abby and Naomi

Thanks for keeping me inspired.

"Paris is not a city; it's a world."
— *King Francis I*

[1]

June, 2011

Horace Artemus Hawthorn IV stumbled down the sidewalk fifteen yards ahead of Wolfgang. In spite of the stiff breeze that ripped through the city, sweat streamed down the polished face of the fourth-generation Chicago aristocrat, outlining his red-rimmed eyes. Every few steps, Hawthorn caught himself against the glass face of a high-dollar storefront. He dropped his briefcase and wiped his forehead, dislodging the eight-hundred-dollar Gucci eyeglasses he wore as he struggled for balance.

Wolfgang stopped on the sidewalk and passed his own briefcase to his free hand, giving Hawthorn a moment to collect himself. The briefcase was identical to the one Hawthorn carried, albeit empty, and Wolfgang felt a little conspicuous carrying it.

Who even uses briefcases anymore?

Crowds of bustling Chicagoans surged around them, passing Hawthorn with no more notice than if he had been a panhandler. Wolfgang adjusted the light jacket he wore, feeling the weight of the package strapped to his lower back. It bit into his skin and chafed with every stride, but the close proximity to his body kept the package invisible to the naked eye. That was lucky, because if any one of the half dozen cops he had passed in the last half hour detected the package, Wolfgang would have earned a one-way ticket to prison faster than he could sneeze.

Hawthorn swabbed his forehead with a handkerchief—something Wolfgang figured only truly rich people carried—and then adjusted his glasses. He recovered his briefcase from the sidewalk and started forward again. His shoulders were squared in the resolute stature of a man who believed himself to be self-made, regardless of the silver spoon he was born clutching. With each stride, he stared directly over the heads of the meaningless worker bees that surged past him—mere pawns in the game of empire of which he was a key player. But in spite of Hawthorn's confident stride and condescending glare, there was a tremor in his knees and an uncertainty to his steps that couldn't be hidden. It was an odd dichotomy to the strange and unexpected euphoria that Wolfgang knew Hawthorn had experienced over the past three weeks.

Heroin is a hell of a drug. Especially when you don't know you're taking it.

Wolfgang hurried after Hawthorn, checking his watch as he slipped among the bustling pedestrians.

It had been seven minutes since Hawthorn left the coffee shop. Each morning, he left his thirtieth-story condo in the Millennium Centre tower and took a private car to his favorite coffee shop, where a dark roast with two creams and one sugar awaited him. He sat near the window, where all the peasants of the world could stare longingly at his sculpted jawline and premium Armani-clad physique, and made a show of reading the *Chicago Tribune*.

Wolfgang doubted whether Hawthorn could read at all, but for a rising star in the powerhouse world of business, appearance was everything.

After consuming the coffee, Hawthorn trashed the paper and walked two blocks to the office suite of Hawthorn and Company, a multi-billion-dollar real estate firm founded by his great-grandfather over a century before, now located on the eightieth floor of the Willis Tower.

And there, encased in an oak panel office, sitting behind the Rolls Royce of desks, the young master of the universe planned the development and destruction of a real estate empire worth more than a small country.

That was a typical day for Hawthorn, but today was anything save typical. Today Hawthorn was destined to spearhead his very first major deal—the eight-hundred-million-dollar acquisition of a rival firm based out of Houston. It was young Hawthorn's first foray into the serious business usually managed exclusively by his father, Hawthorn III, and it marked his initiation as the future CEO of the company.

This was why Hawthorn plowed on toward the Willis Tower, in spite of the chills that racked his body and the dizziness that sent him stumbling into walls. After all, heroin *is* a hell of a drug, and you can't just blindly ingest it for three weeks and then cut yourself off two days before the biggest meeting of your life.

Too bad Hawthorn didn't know he'd been ingesting it. The doses had been small—just frequent and powerful enough to give him a jolt of jollies, yet innocent enough to be dismissed as the thrill of impending corporate stardom. When Wolfgang cut off the supply a little over forty hours before, the loss hadn't been noticed. Not until now, anyway. Now, the rages of withdrawal were in full effect, clouding Hawthorn's mind and jeopardizing his entire future.

Wolfgang remained close enough to keep Hawthorn in sight, but far enough that nobody would take note. The cold sidewalks of downtown Chicago passed beneath him amid a clamor of car horns and shouting voices, but it was easy to keep Hawthorn in sight all the way up to the front steps of the mighty Willis Tower.

Formerly the Sears Building, the Willis Tower was the tallest building in Chicago and the third tallest building in America. Jutting almost fifteen hundred feet into the sky, it loomed over downtown Chicago like a domineering emphasis dedicated to the gods of the corporate universe—which it pretty much was.

Hawthorn stumbled up the front steps toward the glass canopy entrance of the tower. Tourists from around the world were already crowding toward the building, eager to experience the breathtaking view from the tower's observation deck. Hawthorn ignored them, pausing at the door and suddenly clutching one hand over his stomach.

Wolfgang checked his watch. Nine minutes and eighteen seconds had elapsed since Hawthorn left the coffee shop, which meant that his present gut distress was right on schedule. Wolfgang closed the distance between them as Hawthorn pushed through the door and stepped into the massive lobby. More tourists and suit-clad businessmen hid Wolfgang from view as he followed Hawthorn toward the elevator.

But Hawthorn never made it to the elevator. He came within two paces, then doubled over, gripping his stomach. A moment later, he spun on his heel and bolted toward the lobby bathrooms, waddling like an old man with stiff knees—because a laxative is also a hell of a drug and virtually undetectable when mixed in a dark roast with two creams and one sugar.

Wolfgang turned to follow, his shoulders loosening as his stress level began to subside. The operation was all but over now. Hawthorn blasted through the door into the lobby-level bathrooms, and Wolfgang followed two strides behind. The bathroom was bright, with light gleaming off of porcelain sinks and polished mirrors. Banks of bathroom stalls lined the right-hand wall, and Hawthorn made for the first one, sliding through the door like a baseball player skidding onto home plate. The door smacked shut, the briefcase hit the floor, and then Hawthorn hit the throne.

Wolfgang winced at the sounds erupting from the stall. He dug beneath the collar of his dress shirt and produced a stretchy neck gaiter, passing it across his mouth and nose to help block out the smell as he slipped into the stall adjacent to Hawthorn's. Wolfgang kicked the seat cover down over the toilet and sat down as Hawthorn grunted and groaned like a cow giving birth. His hand smacked against the side of the wall as though he were retching, and then another wave of bodily ejections erupted inside Hawthorn's stall.

Wolfgang grimaced and tried to hold his breath. He dug a pair of rubber surgical gloves from his pocket and tugged them on, wishing he could pull them over his head instead. Then he peeked beneath the edge of the stall. Hawthorn's briefcase was visible, standing next to the toilet, only inches from Wolfgang's fingers. He waited until Hawthorn retched and groaned again, then quickly swapped his briefcase for Hawthorn's.

Wolfgang produced a small case from his pocket and snapped it open over his knees. Two electronic plates were inside, connected by wires. The plates featured tiny LED screens on the top sides, with three rubber wheels and a rubber thumb on the bottom side. Wolfgang lifted the plates out of the case and fitted them over the locking dials on the briefcase. The rubber wheels landed perfectly over the metal dials of the briefcase's combination lock, sucking tight against it with magnetic force, and the rubber thumb pressed against the lock switch. He checked to ensure that the device was properly aligned, then hit the only button on either plate.

A soft whirring began a moment later, and numbers flashed across the LED screens as the device began to spin the dials while the rubber thumbs maintained pressure on the lock switches. It checked twenty-eight possible combinations every second as the right-hand device worked backward from 999 and the left worked upward from 000.

It was almost certain that both combinations were the same, so as soon as one device found a winning number, the second device would cease its search and attempt the same number on the opposite side. Most people set the combinations of both sides to the same number, and Hawthorn was anything but a security genius.

Wolfgang leaned back and crossed his arms, waiting and trying not to breathe. Seconds ticked by, and then the left-hand lock popped open with a soft click. 317. Wolfgang tried not to roll his eyes. He should have guessed that number. It was Hawthorn's birthday.

The right-hand plate attempted the same combination a second later, and the lock popped open. He pocketed the device, his fingers moving in a blur as he reached into his coat and unclipped the package from his lower back.

The pod that he produced from beneath his coat wasn't much bigger than a cell phone, but about four times as thick and worth infinitely more. Wolfgang opened it at the same time he opened the briefcase, and carefully deposited its contents inside. Heroin. A lot of heroin. Enough to get Hawthorn slapped with an intent-to-distribute charge.

Wolfgang clicked the briefcase shut amid another round of groans from Hawthorn, and then swapped it with his own again. Then he straightened, flushed the toilet in case anybody was observing him, and exited the stall. After conducting a perfunctory wash of his hands, he walked back through the lobby and into the crisp Chicago air, drawing his phone and punching in a number from memory. The phone rang twice before an elderly male voice answered.

"Hello?"

Wolfgang would have known he was talking to an old WASP by the tone of that word alone.

"Mr. Dudley, my name is Richard Greeley. I'm with the *Wall Street Journal*."

"How the hell did you get this number?"

"I'm working on a story involving your company's merger with Hawthorn and Co and was wondering if you had a comment on Horace Hawthorn's drug problem. Will it be a consideration in the final negotiations?"

"Drug problem? I don't know what you're talking about."

"*The Daily* reported on it just this morning, Mr. Dudley. You *are* involved in final negotiations, are you not?"

The phone clicked off, and Wolfgang lowered it from his ear, shooting off a quick message to a contact labeled only as "E."

Operation complete.

Less than a minute passed before a reply lit up the screen.

B&B. 3.

The Baker and Bean Café and Coffee Shop sat on the edge of downtown, close enough to Lake Michigan that the waterfront wind wafted away the smell of coffee and pastries, replacing it with an odor a lot more fishy and a lot less appetizing. Somebody probably thought it was a great idea to put a cutesy coffee joint this close to the water, but like most contrived attempts at "old-fashioned simplicity," it didn't really work.

Wolfgang was okay with that. He drank little coffee, and he wasn't hungry anyway, so he didn't have an appetite to be spoiled by the acrid odor of diesel fumes and fish guts. Nonetheless, he ordered a water because a man sitting alone in a coffee shop with no drink drew more attention than he wanted.

Edric arrived seventeen minutes late, which Wolfgang expected. Edric had probably been on scene for the better part of an hour but was willing to let Wolfgang sit by himself—exposed—long enough to flush out any possible assassins.

"It's Chicago, Eddie," Wolfgang said as the older man slipped up to the table with an oversized jacket draped over one shoulder. "Nobody is waiting to kill us."

Edric sat down, allowing the coat to slide off his shoulder and into his lap, exposing a white cast encasing his right arm from his shoulder to his wrist. Wolfgang sat up, but Edric held up a cautioning finger.

"What have I told you about that?"

Wolfgang sighed and rolled his eyes. "Act. Never react."

"That's right. It should've been a red flag when I walked in here wearing a coat in early June. Why wasn't it?"

"Because you're my boss," Wolfgang said. "And because I'm wearing a coat. Because people wear coats in Chicago all times of the year, and because I really don't care. What happened to you, anyway?"

Edric waved his good arm dismissively as the server approached.

"What can I get you?" she asked, barely glancing at Edric as her gaze swept Wolfgang from ankle to forehead.

Wolfgang winked at her, a grin creeping across his face.

"Dark house roast," Edric said, shooting Wolfgang a glare. "Black."

She walked off, her hips swaying beneath her apron. Wolfgang followed those hips with his eyes until they disappeared behind the counter.

Edric snapped the fingers on his good hand. "What the hell is wrong with you?"

Wolfgang shrugged, leaned back, and interlaced his fingers behind his head. "Based on my physiological reaction to that ass, I'd say all systems are fully operational. What's wrong with *you*?"

Edric leaned back, rubbing his chin as his

bandaged arm rested on his thigh. He stared Wolfgang down for a long moment, then sighed. "Debrief."

Wolfgang closed his eyes and cocked his head until his neck cracked. "Hawthorn is a heroin addict, but he doesn't know it, and he's currently enjoying some aggressive withdrawals. I phoned a tip to the lead partner of the company out of Houston. When he sees Hawthorn sweating bullets today, he'll connect the dots. At some point, the heroin in Hawthorn's briefcase will be discovered, and the deal will collapse. Mission accomplished." Wolfgang rattled off the answer in relaxed monotone, his gaze drifting back to the server about halfway through.

She set the coffee on the table and smiled at Wolfgang with a little scrunch of her nose—some kind of cutesy gesture, he supposed—then disappeared again.

Edric ignored the coffee and stared Wolfgang down. "Why heroin?"

"What?"

"Why did you select heroin?"

"Oh, you know. I'm using cocaine now, but I had some heroin in my sock drawer. Does it matter?"

Edric made a production of rubbing his eyes with his good hand. "Yes, it matters. Depending on the drug and how you sourced it, that could be a weakness in the operation—a hole that could be exploited if somebody started poking around. Unless, of course, you actually *are* taking drugs..."

"Are you kidding me? I'm not on drugs. What's wrong with you? I bought the heroin off a dealer in Detroit. It's not traceable. Hawthorn is a walking idiot, and nobody is going to question his addiction. Frankly, I'm surprised he wasn't already using. My god, Edric. You get more suspicious all the time."

Edric slowly tapped his finger on the table, still staring Wolfgang down. "What's up with you, Wolf?"

"What are you talking about?"

"You're not . . . sharp. You're not focused."

"Sure I am."

"No, you're not."

"Prove it."

"Today, you took the bus to Hawthorn's coffee shop. I was sitting two benches back, dressed as an old man with a cane, reading a novel. You never saw me."

Wolfgang laughed. "The old man reading the novel was Asian. You should know that because you were sitting at the bus stop where he boarded, feeding pigeons out of a bread bag. Seriously, Edric. Maybe *you're* losing focus."

Edric continued tapping his finger, his stare unbroken.

Wolfgang sighed and threw up one hand. "What?"

"You're bored, aren't you?"

Wolfgang shook his head, then hesitated and shrugged. "Maybe a little."

"You're getting sloppy. Have been for weeks."

"Maybe," Wolfgang admitted.

"Why?"

Wolfgang searched for the server, then sighed. "It's been three years, Edric. I guess . . . I don't know. I just thought the work would be more exciting."

"When I recruited you for SPIRE, I promised you travel, money, and danger. Have I not delivered?"

"You have," Wolfgang said. "Maybe I just need a little more of each."

Wolfgang thought back to Edric's recruitment speech three years before, when he talked with animation about the mysterious company he worked for. SPIRE: a private espionage service specializing in subterfuge, procurement, infiltration, retaliation, and entrapment. At the time, Wolfgang was eighteen, and it all sounded very thrilling, but dumping a laxative in a business executive's coffee felt more junior high than espionage elite, regardless of how effective the strategy was.

"A little more of each," Edric repeated, his voice trailing. "Drugs or no drugs, you have to admit, that's something an addict would say."

Wolfgang didn't dispute the accusation. Excitement was its own form of drug, and like any high, everything dulled after a while. "I don't know, Edric. Just give me another op. Something tropical. I need a tan."

Seconds ticked into minutes while Edric continued to stare, then he seemed to reach a decision. "Does the name 'Charlie Team' mean anything to you?"

Wolfgang shook his head. "Video game?"

"No, it's one of SPIRE's elite team units."

Wolfgang frowned. "What do you mean, team units? SPIRE only hires individual operators."

Edric shrugged. "For petty corporate ops like the Hawthorn job, sure. But sometimes those operators turn out to be exemplary. And sometimes a job is too big for one man."

"What are you telling me?"

"In addition to being your handler, I'm the operation commander of Charlie Team. We execute covert operations on behalf of SPIRE around the world. Next-level stuff. Stuff with a lot more risk and a lot more reward."

Wolfgang remained relaxed, trying to disguise the twitch he felt in his stomach.

Edric held his gaze, then picked up the coffee and took a long sip. "Charlie Team is fully operational, with five members—myself, a techie, and three ground-level operators. Three weeks ago, we conducted an operation in Damascus and things went sideways. One of my guys was killed, and I was thrown off a building. Hence the cast."

Wolfgang sat forward involuntarily. He could tell where this conversation was headed, and he was already sold.

"I received a call from the director this morning. He's got a special job that he wants Charlie Team to take. I can lead from behind, given the cast, but I can't get by without three operators on the ground. I need somebody new. Somebody . . . exemplary."

Wolfgang flipped a twenty-dollar bill out of his pocket and pinned it beneath his water.

"Lucky you. I'm free this weekend."

[2]

The setting sun gleamed against The Gateway Arch as Wolfgang stepped out of the cab and passed the driver a fifty. The driver fumbled for change, and Wolfgang waved him off, taking a moment to admire the old monument. A haze of pollution clouded it, and shabby buildings blocked part of his view, but it was still something worth admiring.

Wolfgang had never been to St. Louis before. He wasn't sure if this was SPIRE's headquarters or if Edric simply deemed it to be the most convenient location for Charlie Team's next rendezvous. The cryptic, encoded text message from the previous night directed him to fly into St. Louis and meet on the fourteenth floor of the Bank of America Plaza at seven p.m. It was now barely five-thirty, but Wolfgang believed in arriving early. It gave him an advantage over whatever kind of initiation awaited him.

He had the cab drop him off six blocks north of Eighth and Market Street, choosing to walk the final stretch to acclimate himself to the city. There wasn't much to see on a Saturday afternoon—apparently, most of the St. Louis downtown action orbited around business, not tourism. Only a few people bustled past him on the dirty sidewalks, although he counted at least thirty panhandlers, along with two distant gunshots.

St. Louis—not exactly a family town.

Wolfgang arrived at the Bank of America Plaza without breaking a sweat, but still appreciated the air conditioning inside. His shoes clicked against marble floors, echoing inside an empty lobby as he moved toward the elevator. There was a security guard at the front desk watching Netflix on an iPad, and he made no effort to stop or question Wolfgang before the elevator door closed.

Wolfgang pressed the button for the sixteenth floor and stuck his hands into his pockets, contemplating all the things that could happen. Prior to the previous day, he really had no idea that SPIRE operated multi-person units, but it shouldn't have surprised him. His three-year tenure with the peculiar, independent espionage service had led him all over North America, mostly conducting petty sabotage and intellectual theft jobs against corporations, not governments. The prior day's operation was a prime example—somebody didn't want the Hawthorn and Company deal to close, and they were willing to pay handsomely to have it sabotaged. So they hired SPIRE, and SPIRE deployed Wolfgang, and Wolfgang got creative and made it happen. Boring, really.

When Edric recruited Wolfgang to work for SPIRE just months prior to his eighteenth birthday, Wolfgang had dreamed of fast jets, flying bullets, and exotic locales. So far, his average mission was more likely to land him in Cleveland than Bangladesh. Hardly the stuff of James Bond movies.

The elevator dinged to a stop on the sixteenth floor, and Wolfgang stepped into the lobby. Offices for a construction firm lay to his right, and more elevators to his left. The entire floor was dark and silent, fast asleep after a busy week.

He stepped out of the elevator and slipped his hand into his coat, feeling for the Beretta 92X Compact handgun held in a shoulder holster beneath his left armpit. Wolfgang kept his hand on the gun as he stepped to the stairwell and eased the door open, listening for any sounds from two floors beneath him.

As he expected, all was silent. He really didn't foresee any games from Edric; he wasn't the game-playing type. But then again, twenty-four hours before, Wolfgang hadn't expected to be recruited to an unknown team, either. He wasn't about to walk in with his pants down.

He took a cautious step into the stairwell, then crept down two flights of stairs and into the lobby of the fourteenth floor. All was silent, and Wolfgang adjusted his grip on the pistol, then took a cautious step down the hallway.

"Hey, moron! Over here."

Wolfgang jumped and whirled around.

An office door, half-hidden behind a decorative tree at the corner of the lobby, swung open, and Edric leaned out. He shot Wolfgang a glare, then jerked his head toward the room behind him. "You're early," Edric said as Wolfgang sheepishly withdrew his hand from his coat.

"Early is alive," Wolfgang said.

It was one of Edric's favorite quips, and Wolfgang hoped it would win him some points for being caught with his back turned.

Edric didn't seem to care. He just stepped back, allowing Wolfgang to slide into the room, then the door smacked shut.

The office suite was laid out like a penthouse, minus the fancy trappings or expensive furniture. A wall of windows stared out over the Mississippi River and the Gateway Arch, while a hodgepodge of folding chairs, a cheap futon, and a beanbag were strewn over the industrial carpet.

On one wall was a massive marker board,

currently festooned with a series of completed tic-tac-toe games, and in the middle of the room was a folding table with a few chairs gathered around it. The only light in the room shone in from the windows, growing gradually dimmer as the sun faded behind the tower.

Three people looked up as Wolfgang shuffled in. First was a tall man with broad shoulders and the kind of buzzed haircut that only an ex-military guy would subject himself to. He had milky blue eyes, and from the moment Wolfgang caught his gaze, he felt unwelcome. Buzzcut stood next to the windows and raised one eyebrow in condescending dismissal.

A second man was short and wiry, with long fingers and round glasses that sat on a sharp nose. His black T-shirt was covered with bleach stains, and he leaned over a laptop computer as though it were his child, not even looking up as Wolfgang entered.

Then there was the petite woman sitting in a corner. Wolfgang didn't notice her at first. She leaned back against the wall with her legs crossed and a cocktail glass in one hand. Shadows played across her face, obscuring her features, but it was impossible to miss the bright red of her hair, which was held back in a ponytail and laid over one shoulder. Eyes closed, she looked perfectly relaxed, as if the world around her either existed or it didn't, and either way, she wasn't going to move.

Wolfgang felt Buzzcut's glare and realized he'd

been staring. Somehow, the irritation of the big man only made him want to stare longer.

Edric cleared his throat. "Drink?"

"Sprite," Wolfgang said.

Edric retrieved a beer and a can of Sprite from a mini-fridge, then hit a switch on the wall. The room flooded with bright LED light from overhead, and Wolfgang could now see the woman in perfect clarity.

She was attractive. She kept her eyes closed, apparently undisturbed by the glare. Her face reminded him of a china doll, with rounded cheeks and a nose that was more of the button variety than the supermodel shape, but suited her perfectly.

She was cute more than hot. Pretty more than runway gorgeous. The kind of woman you might just as soon meet in Iowa as you would Los Angeles, but she'd draw eyes either way. Wolfgang liked that for some reason. Something about the way she gently pulled herself to her feet and turned to the window, stretching and running a hand through her hair was confident but weary, as if she hadn't slept much lately or had something heavy on her mind.

Whatever it was, it kept him staring far longer than was polite.

"Hey, shitface. Shut your mouth before I stick a brick in it."

Wolfgang turned toward Buzzcut, whose eyes blazed somewhere between disgust and irritation.

Wolfgang smirked, a retort already wavering on his lips as Edric pressed the Sprite into his hand.

"Ease up, Kev," Edric said. "Let's be friendly." He snapped his fingers and motioned to the table.

Wolfgang glanced back in time to see the woman take one more look out the window before turning to the table, and then he saw her eyes. They were large and grey, a little brighter than stone, and crystal clear, but sad. As she brushed hair away from her face and scrunched her nose, he saw a deep pain accentuated by a slight redness in her cheeks. Their gazes met, and in an instant, the sadness vanished, replaced by a block wall. Her back stiffened, and she looked away, proceeding to the table without giving him a second look.

"Have a seat, Wolf," Edric said. He motioned to the end of the table as the woman and Buzzcut found their seats.

Wolfgang slid into the end chair and took a long pull of the Sprite, suddenly feeling very awkward and self-conscious.

"All right, everybody," Edric said. He stepped behind Wolfgang and gave him a slap on the shoulder. "This is Wolfgang Pierce. He's been with the company for three years, and he's now joining Charlie Team."

The woman picked at her fingernails, and the wiry man behind the computer continued to stare at his screen. Only Buzzcut faced Wolfgang, his eyes as cold as death.

Man, what's up this guy's ass?

Edric walked around the table and smacked the laptop shut without ceremony. The wiry man opened his mouth to object, but Edric continued.

"Wolfgang, welcome to Charlie Team. On your left is Kevin Jones. Besides being a three-time world champion of the Resting Bitch Face Olympics, Kevin is our primary driver and combat specialist. When we need the big guns, Kevin's our man."

Wolfgang nodded once at Kevin but received nothing more than a continued glare.

Edric moved around the table. "Center stage is Lyle Tillman. Lyle is our tech wizard. Phones, computers, security, communications, high-tech gadgets . . . Lyle makes it happen."

Wolfgang offered the nod to Lyle and was gratified to have the wiry man return it, even if he wouldn't meet Wolfgang's gaze. Edric moved toward the woman, and Wolfgang felt self-conscious again.

"Last but not least is Megan Rudolph. Megan is our senior operator and Charlie Team's second-in-command. Her specialties include interrogation, infiltration, and operations coordination. Prior to working for SPIRE, she worked for the FBI. If Megan says jump, you say how high. Got it?"

Wolfgang flashed what he hoped was a friendly smile. "Pleasure to meet you."

Kevin stiffened, but Megan looked up. She appraised Wolfgang with a quick sweep of those brilliant grey eyes, her lips lifting in a perfunctory smile, and Wolfgang adjusted his assessment again. Megan was more than cute; she was beautiful. Not in an ordinary way, certainly, but that smile, however brief and stiff, lit up the room like a flare.

She returned her gaze to her fingernails, and the smile faded as quickly as it had come. Wolfgang swallowed and chugged his Sprite.

"Okay, then," Edric said. "I realize the circumstances around Wolfgang's recruitment are rushed and unusual, but—"

"We don't need him," Kevin growled. "It's a liability having somebody we don't know. I don't like it."

Edric's tone remained calm. "I hear you, Kev, but we do need him. I'm out of the field until my arm heals, and you and Megan can't operate alone."

"Is he trained?" Lyle's voice was as mousy as his appearance—little more than a squeak.

"Yes," Edric said. "Like I said, he's a three-year veteran of SPIRE's corporate espionage division."

"So, he's got no experience with a team," Kevin said. "He shouldn't be here."

Edric set his beer down and leaned over the table, wrapping his fingers over the back of a chair.

"Look. I hear you. But this is happening. If you're not comfortable with it, you can leave. Okay?"

Kevin shot Wolfgang a long glower, then looked at Megan. She was still busy picking her fingernails, but she looked up and swept another passive gaze over Wolfgang, every bit as quick as she had the first time. He felt her look in his bones—sharp and penetrating—and he had the distinct impression that she was evaluating him on a molecular level, like an X-ray that searched for weaknesses in his body language. The experience was maddening, but something about her attention was addictive, too.

Megan nodded once, and Kevin grunted and folded his arms.

"Okay, then." Edric wiped away the tic-tac-toe games from the marker board, then selected a red marker and began to write.

"We're going to Paris. Bravo Team was originally tasked, but the director reassigned the operation last minute. So, the pressure's on . . . got me?"

Edric wrote *Paris* across the top of the board, then turned to the table. "Our primary objective is an unknown male, code-named Spider. He's an anarchist suspected of running a complex, multi-national terrorist organization. His ethnicity, background, and true identity are all unknown. The CIA has been tracking him for the past six months and believe that his organization is preparing a terrorist attack for someplace in Western Europe."

"Why?" Kevin asked.

Edric wrote "Spider - ID unknown" on the

whiteboard. "Why what?"

"Why the attack?" Kevin said. "What's his motive?"

"He's an anarchist," Edric said with a little shrug, as if that explained it. "Captured manifestos from his organization call for the dismantlement of all governments around the world. Basically, anarchists want chaos. They believe it will 'restore natural balance' to the planet. Whatever that means."

"So, we're gonna take him out?" Kevin asked. There was a hint of a smile on the edge of his lips that sent a chill down Wolfgang's spine.

Edric shook his head. "Negative. In fact, our mission is to protect him."

"What the hell?" Kevin's eyebrows furrowed, but Wolfgang's mind was spinning, already unraveling the puzzle.

"The CIA is in contact with him," Wolfgang said. "They need intel."

Edric pointed the marker toward Wolfgang. "Bingo. The CIA has an operator, code-named Raven, who has established contact with Spider and is slowly gaining his trust. Spider is meeting Raven in Paris thirty-six hours from now. The CIA hopes this meeting will provide critical intel about Spider's identity, his operations, and the attack he's planning."

Edric returned to the whiteboard and wrote "CIA" on it, with an arrow connecting "CIA" and "Spider."

"Wait . . . You said we were protecting Spider, though," Kevin said. "From who?"

Wolfgang wondered the same thing.

Edric wrote another word on the whiteboard, completing a triangle with lines connecting the new word. "Russia," he said, stepping back from the board. "The Russian Foreign Intelligence Service has been tracking Spider also, and they've obtained his plans to meet a foreign operator in Paris. As far as we know, the Russians are clueless as to the CIA operation, and we need to keep it that way. However, if we know anything about our friends from Moscow, they aren't likely to ask questions. We suspect they've already deployed a hit team to eliminate Spider and prevent his planned attack."

"But if they succeed, we'll never know where the attack was planned to take place, or who else was behind it," Wolfgang said. He leaned forward, his mind racing as he connected the dots. "We need more than Spider. We need the people behind him. The financing, the foot soldiers, the weapons suppliers."

"Cha-ching. Exactly," Edric said. "The CIA needs intel from Spider, and they'll never get it if Moscow guns him down. So, we have to protect Spider—at least until the CIA is finished with him."

"Why can't the CIA protect him themselves?" Kevin asked.

"Plausible deniability," Wolfgang said. "Spider is

a global terrorist, and the US isn't on great terms with Russia. If they discovered the CIA protecting a known anarchist, Russia could easily spin their hit squad as a policing team sent to detain Spider, and then frame the CIA as collaborating with him. It would be an international scandal. The CIA needs a third party to shield Spider. Somebody they can disavow."

The room fell quiet, and Wolfgang noticed that everybody seemed to be waiting on Megan to speak. She sat still, staring at him with piercing, unblinking eyes. Then she nodded once, and the gesture sent a strange jolt of elation shooting through Wolfgang.

Edric replaced the cap on his marker. "Right again. The CIA needs distance. Also, France is a sovereign nation. The CIA can't deploy an armed commando force into downtown Paris uninvited. That's a serious breach of international ethics."

"The Russians are doing it," Lyle said.

Kevin snorted. "The Russians don't give a shit about international ethics."

"They really don't," Edric said. "Which is why we can expect a fight if things go sideways." He set the marker down and scratched his injured arm beneath the edge of the cast.

Wolfgang drained the rest of the Sprite. *Paris. Russian hit teams. Intriguing teammates.* Charlie Team was looking like a heck of a good idea, regardless of Kevin and his RBF.

"Okay, then." Edric smacked his cast with his good hand. "Our mission is to fly to Paris and find Spider before the Russians do, then protect him until he completes his rendezvous with Raven. We'll be armed, but ideally, we pull this off without any fireworks. I'm setting operational protocols at Code Orange."

Wolfgang raised a finger, and Kevin rolled his eyes.

"Oh, for heaven's sake. He doesn't even know the protocol codes."

"Calm down, Kevin," Edric said. He turned to Wolfgang. "We have three levels of engagement: yellow, orange, and red. Yellow means we're unarmed. Orange means we carry guns, but we don't shoot unless we're shot at."

"And red?" Wolfgang asked.

Edric laughed a little. "Red means Kevin takes over."

Lyle and Kevin joined in on the laugh.

Edric rested his hands on the back of the nearest chair. "When we reach Paris, Kevin, Megan, and Wolfgang will be on the ground. Lyle and I will remain in the rear, running communications and surveillance. Questions?"

Nobody said a word.

Edric grinned. "All right, then. Let's go save a terrorist."

[3]

"Holy cow," Wolfgang whispered. "Am I getting a pay raise with this job?"

Hot summer wind whipped across his face as he shut the door of the taxi and stared out across the tarmac. A Gulfstream G550 jet sat on the private runway outside of St. Louis, the engine already running at idle, with the door open and the steps resting on the concrete.

"Private espionage is high-paying work," Edric said. "When you're the best, you get the best toys."

He tossed Wolfgang a duffle bag loaded with what felt like bricks and started toward the plane. Wolfgang followed as Kevin and Megan ran up the steps carrying similar backpacks. Lyle struggled behind them, wheeling two heavy cases full of what Wolfgang assumed to be computer equipment.

Wolfgang shouldered the duffle and turned back, holding out his hand. "Here. Let me help."

Lyle blinked up at him from behind smudged glasses. He reluctantly surrendered one of his precious cases, and the two started toward the plane.

"Thanks," Lyle said. "Nobody ever helps with my gear."

"I don't mind," Wolfgang said. "What have you got here, anyway?"

Lyle's eyes flashed, and Wolfgang wondered if he'd regret asking.

"Everything we need," Lyle said. "Communications, surveillance, infiltration equipment. It's just like the movies. I've got all the gadgets."

Wolfgang laughed. "Got any X-ray glasses?"

Lyle stopped mid-stride and squinted up at Wolfgang. "X-ray glasses?"

Wolfgang grinned. "You know. Glasses that let you see through stuff. Walls . . . doors . . . clothes . . ." He winked and tilted his head toward the plane.

Lyle wrinkled his nose before his gaze turned cold, and he snatched the second case from Wolfgang's grasp. Without a word, he set off in a quick march, wheeling both cases behind him.

"Hey!" Wolfgang said. "What did I say? It was just a joke, man."

Wolfgang hurried up the steps as Lyle clattered ahead, dragging his cases and disappearing into the plane. The cabin of the aircraft smelled faintly of an ocean breeze air freshener. Wolfgang had to duck to step inside, and he stared down an interior featuring plush leather chairs, a minibar, and a door at the back that he guessed led to bunks.

The others were already gathered around the middle of the cabin, pivoting their chairs to face each other.

"Wolf, hurry it up," Edric said, waving his cast-frozen arm.

Wolfgang slid into the nearest chair, casting a casual glance around the cabin. He'd never flown first class, let alone private. The aircraft was small, but with only five of them on board, it felt like Air Force One.

Lyle took a seat in the back, pushing his glasses up his nose. Kevin sat in the middle, dressed in cargo pants and a black shirt that was two sizes too small, accentuating a six-pack that would make Chuck Norris envious. He glared at Wolfgang, then looked away as if the newcomer wasn't worth his attention.

Megan, next to a window, had a closed sketchpad and a stick of charcoal in her lap. She stared out the window absently, her scarlet hair swept behind one ear.

Wolfgang watched her a moment and wondered what was in the sketchpad. He knew next to nothing about art but was intrigued by the idea that Megan might be an artist.

"Hey! New guy!" Kevin's chunky fingers

snapped in front of Wolfgang's face. "Are you retarded or what? Stop gawking."

Wolfgang felt a vague irritation and brushed Kevin's hand away but said nothing. He was still thinking about Megan. Still wondering what lay behind those grey eyes.

"Don't say *retard*, Kevin," Megan said in a soft voice with just a hint of rasp. "It's not acceptable anymore."

Wolfgang realized it was the first time she'd said anything in his presence.

Kevin flushed and leaned back, his glare darkening to a scowl.

"That's enough, all of you." Edric settled into his seat as the plane's door hissed shut and the aircraft began to move. He held a glass with a pool of liquor swimming in the bottom, his broken arm held close to his side.

Wolfgang noticed him wincing as he settled into the plush seat and took a sip.

"All right. Eyes front, everybody."

Wolfgang tore his focus away from Megan and sat up. He felt the blistering wrath of Kevin directed his way and shot the bigger man a wink and a grin. Kevin looked ready to explode.

Edric produced a file from the seat next to him, opened it, and passed photos around the circle. They were black-and-white distance shots of a tall man in a business suit with black hair and a bold jaw. He appeared to be Caucasian but sported a tan so dark he may have been of Italian or Greek descent.

"This is Raven," Edric said. "He's currently in the air on the way to rendezvous with Spider. Our communication with Raven will be highly limited on the ground. The CIA doesn't want him to wear any direct communications equipment in case Spider searches him."

Wolfgang stared at the face as the plane gained speed and the wheels left the ground. The deep eyes of the man in the photograph were penetrating, but not uncomfortably so. If Wolfgang had to guess, he wouldn't have said that this man was a CIA operative, but maybe that was part of the job description—you had to blend in.

"We also don't know where the meeting is going to take place," Edric continued. "Spider will communicate that information to Raven at the last moment, for security purposes."

Kevin said, "We can't talk to Raven, we don't know where Spider is, and we don't know what he looks like. How the hell are we supposed to pull this off?"

Edric nodded at Megan, who was fixated on the photograph.

"We know when Raven lands, right?" Megan asked.

"Yes," Edric said.

"So, we pick him up at the airport," she said.

"Trail him from there to the meeting spot. Stay in the shadows and look out for both Spider and the Russians. It's not ideal. It leaves us at the vulnerability of whatever terrain Spider chooses. But if we can't communicate with Raven, it'll have to do."

Megan leaned toward the file, her relaxed and disengaged posture of only moments before melting away. Her voice was clear and strong, carrying a hint of command that Wolfgang hadn't noticed before.

Edric smiled. "Very good. That's the plan."

"What about an SDR?" Wolfgang asked, eager to contribute. "Won't Raven run one?"

"SDR?" Kevin said.

"Surveillance detection route," Wolfgang said. "It's a tactic used by covert operatives to shake away anybody trailing them—"

"I know what an SDR is, moron," Kevin said. "Did you miss the part where this guy is working *with* us? He's not trying to shake us."

Megan ran a hand over her eyes. "Don't say *moron*, Kevin."

"Of course Raven doesn't *want* to shake us," Wolfgang said. "But if he's in communication with Spider, and Spider is worried about security, don't you think he might order Raven to conduct an SDR? Raven wouldn't have a choice."

"Wolfgang's right," Edric said. "It's a possibility we have to consider. Raven will do everything he can to keep us with him, but he doesn't know what we look like, and he can't appear to be working with anyone. Unfortunately, we can't put a tracker on him for the same reason we can't put communications on him. So, it's up to us to stick on him like a flea on a dog. We *cannot* lose him. Understood?"

A chorus of grunts passed around the room.

Edric drained the glass. "Good. Everybody familiarize yourselves with some Parisian maps. Lyle and I will be positioned in a van as close to the action as possible. I'll drive and maintain operational control of the mission while Lyle hacks into the Parisian traffic camera network. That should give us an edge on keeping track of Raven. Megan will take point on following him while Wolfgang and Kevin provide direct support. Megan, did you work out some transportation?"

"Yeah. Got us set up with some bikes."

"That should do it. Questions?"

Wolfgang looked back at the photo of Raven, absorbing the facial features staring back at him—the face he couldn't afford to forget.

Edric stood. "Okay, then. Make sure you guys get some sleep." He reached into his coat and produced a glossy travel brochure, then flipped it to Wolfgang with a smirk. "Welcome to Paris, Wolf."

He disappeared into the back of the plane, and Wolfgang studied the brochure. It was an English travel guide to Paris, prominently featuring the Eiffel Tower. He flipped through it, surveying a few paragraphs of tourist lore. He'd never been to Paris before. "The City of Lights," the brochure said, and a city of romance. He glanced over the top of the brochure at Megan. With her notebook now open, her hand moved in gentle arcs across the page, scraping charcoal against the paper.

Kevin snapped his fingers again. "Hey, dum-dum."

Wolfgang looked up and sighed. "Don't do that."

"Do what?"

"Snap your fingers at me. It's really irritating."

"Oh yeah? What you gonna do about it?"

Wolfgang held his gaze, then grinned, lifting his lip just enough to expose some teeth. It was a tactic he'd used before. He called it his "crazy stare," and it never failed him.

Kevin broke after less than twenty seconds, standing up and stomping to the minibar while muttering curses.

Wolfgang stood up also, tapping the brochure against his fingers, and stepped across the cabin toward Megan. His stomach felt suddenly unstable, as if an ocean were swimming inside. "What are you drawing?" he asked.

Megan continued to sketch, her body language tensed and focused.

Wolfgang fiddled with the brochure. "I mean, I don't want to pry. I just like art. Maybe when we get to Paris we'll have some time to see some paintings. Have you ever been to the Louvre?"

Without looking up, Megan drew a slow breath and swept a stray strand of hair behind her ear. "Do you have questions?" Her voice was calm but all business.

He frowned. "Questions? I just thought we could get to know—"

"About the operation. Do you have questions about the operation?"

"Oh." The ocean in his stomach froze over instantly. "No. I think I'm good."

"That's great. You should probably get some sleep. This is gonna be a high-energy job."

Wolfgang could feel Lyle's and Kevin's eyes on him. "Right. Of course." He turned toward the tail of the plane.

The engines roared outside, reduced to a loud hum by the thick insulation of the premium fuselage.

Kevin sat at the rear of the cabin, a glass of whiskey in one hand, his lips gleaming with residue from the drink. He grinned as Wolfgang stepped toward the door to the bunks. "Why don't you pour yourself a drink, Wolf? We can get to know each other." The sarcasm in his tone cut like a blade.

Wolfgang stopped at the door and dug his fingernails into the travel brochure before reaching for the handle. "No, thanks. I don't drink."

[4]

The plane touched down a little over ten hours later, the tires squealing against a private airport someplace outside of Paris. Wolfgang slept six or seven hours and spent the rest of the flight studying maps of the big city. It was impossible for him to really absorb so many streets in such a brief period. Paris was huge, sprawling over an area of almost forty-one square miles, packed with over two million people. Finding one man in that mix and keeping track of him through the busy streets for an indefinite period was daunting, to say the least.

Wolfgang changed into a pair of jeans, a T-shirt and a loose leather jacket that allowed for plenty of room to conceal the Beretta in a shoulder holster. Handguns in Paris were highly restricted items, and being caught with one was sure to be a nightmare. But being caught without one while hunting an elusive terrorist amid a team of Russian assassins seemed the greater risk.

Wolfgang stepped out of the plane and shielded his eyes against the bright sunlight that was just breaking over the eastern horizon. There wasn't much around them other than rolling green farmland. The plane sat at the edge of the tarmac near a row of low hangars, and Wolfgang realized he had yet to see or interact with the pilots. He glanced up at the cockpit, then shrugged and hurried to follow the others toward the nearest hangar.

Dusty and dimly lit inside, the cavernous space was empty except for four vehicles—a white Mercedes panel van and three identical motorcycles parked in a neat row, their front wheels all canted to the left.

Lyle headed straight for the van, trailing his cases, and Wolfgang hurried to follow him. He still wasn't sure what he had done to offend the tech wizard, but he didn't want to leave the issue unresolved. If Lyle had all the gadgets and ran all the communications, he wanted to be friends.

Lyle opened the rear door of the van and started to lift the case. Wolfgang grabbed it first and slid it inside, and Lyle squinted up at him from behind his dirty glasses.

"Hey," Wolfgang said. "About last night . . . I just want to say, I meant nothing by it. Bad joke. I appreciate the work you're doing." He offered his hand.

Lyle's gaze switched from Wolfgang's face to his hand, then back again. He chewed his lip a moment, then accepted the offered hand with a surprisingly strong grip. "Come here. I've got something for you," Lyle said. He ducked into the van, and Wolfgang followed. Lyle flipped a hard plastic case open and produced a tiny earpiece, flicking a switch on before passing it to Wolfgang. "This is your comm. Signal is great, and the mic is sensitive. No need to speak in louder than a conversational tone. Only thing is, the battery life isn't great. Remember to charge it between use."

Wolfgang fit the little device into his right ear canal. It slid in without resistance and was almost comfortable.

Lyle dug into the case and produced another box, sliding the lid off with obvious care and exposing a watch nested inside. At least, it was on a band like a watch, but instead of a round face it had a square face with a black screen. Wolfgang had never seen anything like it.

"And this . . ." Lyle indulged in a brief smile, the first Wolfgang had seen. "This is truly special. I've only got one of them. You can try it out."

"What is it?" Wolfgang asked. "Some kind of watch?"

Lyle lifted the device from the case and passed it to Wolfgang. "It's not a watch. It's a fully purposed spy gadget. I ripped the design off some Apple blueprints. Apparently, they're designing something like it for release in a few years, but I couldn't wait that long. Took me months to perfect it. There's a camera built into the outside of the case, and anything you direct that camera at, I can see. So if you need intel on something, you just show it to me, and I can look it up for you."

"Sweet, man." Wolfgang lifted the watch and wrapped it around his left wrist. It felt great. A little heavy, but not unbearable.

"The true benefit, though," Lyle said, "is in its detection ability. I call it a sniffer. The watch can detect all kinds of poisonous gasses and chemical agents, and it'll give you an alert if there's anything you should be worried about. It even has a built-in Geiger counter."

"Like, for nuclear?" Wolfgang raised one eyebrow, and Lyle nodded eagerly.

"Absolutely. It's not perfect, but it's pretty reliable. Let me know how it works in the field."

Edric's voice boomed from someplace in the hangar. "Hey, Wolf. Get out here!"

Wolfgang slapped Lyle on the shoulder, then piled out of the van. The others were gathered around the bikes, Megan already astride hers. She sat with the easy confidence of a woman who was familiar with fast motorcycles, and Wolfgang couldn't help but stare again.

"Get your comm?" Edric asked.

He scratched his cast again, and Wolfgang realized Edric was probably nervous. This was his first mission since breaking his arm and his first mission with a new operator . . . and without an old one.

Wolfgang tapped his ear. "Right here."

"Very good. We only use radio tags, for extra security. I'm Charlie Lead. Lyle is Charlie Eye, Megan is Charlie One, Kevin is Charlie Two."

Edric paused a moment, and his tone softened. "You're Charlie Three."

Wolfgang saw Megan glance down, and for just a moment, he thought she winced. It was such a small reaction he couldn't be sure, but he thought it corresponded with Edric's mention of Charlie Three.

That was his call sign . . . The guy who died on the last mission.

Wolfgang didn't know what to say, so he just nodded.

"While you're on the ground, you take operational orders from Megan, unless and until I override them. Is that clear?"

Wolfgang nodded again.

"Great. Let's roll."

Edric shuffled to the van, and Wolfgang moved to the bike at the end of the line.

"Can you ride, dum-dum?" Kevin asked.

Wolfgang looked down at the bike, taking a moment to trace his finger down the fuel tank's smooth curve. It was a Triumph Street Triple RS, brand-new, shadow grey with red accents. Identical to the others. He'd never driven a Triumph before but assumed it operated pretty much the same as his Kawasaki back home. "I can ride," he said.

Kevin snorted, then slid his helmet on and flipped up the visor. He turned to Megan. "You good?" His tone was softer but still gruff and condescending.

Megan slapped her visor down without a word and kicked the starter. The bike roared to life, and a second later, she shot out of the hangar like a bullet.

Wolfgang hit the starter and gunned the motor as a shot of adrenaline raced into his blood. This was something new. Something different.

And it was starting right now.

Charles de Gaulle Airport, better known as Roissy Airport, sat twenty miles northeast of downtown Paris. It took them twenty minutes to get there, roaring amid tightly packed morning commuters as they circled the eastern side of the city and approached the airport.

Megan was difficult to keep up with. She pushed the Triumph hard, cutting in and out of trucks and taxis as if she were on a racetrack. Wolfgang was surprised—he would have assumed they would want to avoid attention, not attract it. But there were a lot of motorcycles on the road, many more than in America, and they all drove aggressively. He pushed himself to keep up, taking moderate gratification in Kevin's obvious hesitation to push himself as hard. Apparently, his bark was worse than his bite. At least on a bike.

After reaching the airport, they deposited the Triumphs in short-term parking, leaving the helmets and venturing into the nearest terminal.

Megan spoke over the comm. "Charlie One, I'm taking over ground control. Comm check."

"Charlie Lead, roger ground control assumption. Comms clear."

"Charlie Eye, I have you on satellite." Lyle's voice was squeaky over the earpiece, but at least Wolfgang could hear him clearly.

"Charlie Two, loud and clear."

To Wolfgang's surprise, the arrogance had left Kevin's tone. He spoke with calm focus. Wolfgang shot him a look as he radioed in his own confirmation, and Kevin sneered at him.

"Moving into the terminal now," Megan said. "Charlie Two, take international arrivals from Europe. Charlie Three, you've got North America."

"Copy that." Wolfgang resisted the urge to scratch his ear. Talking made the earpiece move, and it itched now. He feigned a yawn to adjust it, but it only helped a little.

The airport was nothing short of massive.

Tourists and business travelers pressed in on all sides, dragging roll-around suitcases and shouting to each other over their own clamor. There was no dominant nationality. Wolfgang saw Asians, Arabs, South Americans, and Africans as frequently as Europeans. They crushed in on every side, frequently slamming into his shoulders.

How the hell was he supposed to find a single man in this melting pot? He couldn't even see Kevin anymore. His fellow operator had faded like a ghost.

"Dammit, Charlie Three," Megan said. "You're sticking out like a clown. Relax and move to North America."

Wolfgang cast a glance around him, but he couldn't see her. She, too, had faded into the crowd and was now lost from view. He drew a deep breath, which morphed naturally into another yawn. He pretended to pop his neck, then shoved his hands into his pockets and followed the signs toward international arrivals from North America. Everything was written in English as well as French, making navigation easier than he expected.

Dozens of airlines lined up next to each other, pressed together with travelers flooding out of boarding tunnels. Wolfgang assumed a position at the edge of the room, then slid onto a bench and pulled out his phone, retrieving his digital copy of Raven's image. He stared at it a moment, then scanned the room.

"Get me out of your pocket, Charlie Three," Lyle said. "Let me have a look."

Wolfgang frowned in confusion, then recalled the wristwatch. His left hand was still jammed in his pocket. He withdrew it and casually rested his hand against the armrest, exposing the undetectable camera lens to the main lobby of the terminal.

"That's better," Lyle said.

Wolfgang made a mental note to pay specific attention to the position of his left hand next time he went to take a piss, then returned to his surveillance of the lobby. Minutes dragged into half an hour, but he didn't mind. He was used to operations like this. In three years as a lone operator, he'd spent hundreds of hours simply sitting and watching, waiting for something to happen or somebody to show up. It wasn't difficult. It just took practice to remain alert for that long.

The comms remained silent, and Wolfgang twisted his left arm from time to time, panning the watch's camera around the room and giving Lyle an opportunity to detect anything he might have missed. A flight attendant in a form-fitting skirt walked past, and Wolfgang had the momentary, immature urge to follow her with the camera. He recalled Lyle's poor reaction to his last joke and decided against it.

What's up with that, anyway? Why is he so stiff?

Maybe Lyle wasn't stiff. Maybe he was just defensive of Megan. Everybody on the team seemed oddly defensive of Megan. Kevin obviously had a thing for her, which was fine. Wolfgang wasn't threatened. But deeper than that, it was almost as if...

Wolfgang's thoughts were interrupted by a new flood of travelers exiting a nearby gate. A tall man walking in the middle of the crowd, dressed in a black suit with a black overcoat and carrying a briefcase, caught his eye. Wolfgang checked the face against the image on his phone, then cleared his throat. "Charlie One, I have a possible match."

He twisted his left wrist to give Lyle an unobstructed view. "Charlie Eye, can you confirm?"

There was a pause, then Lyle's excited, nasally tone filled the comm. "Positive confirmation. That's Raven."

Wolfgang stood slowly, stretching his back and keeping Raven in his peripheral vision. "Charlie One, I have Raven exiting Delta Flight 7067, direct from New York. Moving to customs."

"Copy that, Charlie Three. I have him."

Edric broke over the comms. "Charlie Lead assuming operation control. Charlie One, stay on him. Charlie Two, Charlie Three, return to transport and stand by."

Wolfgang slid his phone back into his pocket and broke away from the crowds, stepping back through the terminal and into the bright sunlight of the French morning. By the time he made it to his bike,

Kevin was already there, his helmet on and his visor up as the motor rumbled beneath him. Wolfgang slid the helmet over his head and gunned the motor to life, then yawned to adjust the earpiece again.

"Raven is through customs," Megan said. "Staying with him . . ."

Wolfgang felt his heart rate rise, and he twisted his hand around the accelerator, suddenly wishing he'd thought to bring gloves. Even in June, it was cooler in Paris than he expected, and the biting wind on the highway made it worse.

"Raven has taken a black Citroën C5 taxicab," Megan said. "Plate number Lima, Bravo, two, six, five, Lima, Alpha. I've affixed a beacon to the car. Breaking contact now."

Wolfgang felt a buzz in his pocket and withdrew his phone to see an alert flashing on the screen. The GPS link from the beacon had already connected directly to his navigation app. He clipped the phone into the mount between the handlebars and reached for his visor.

"Hey, dum-dum," Kevin said.

Wolfgang shot him an irritated look and detected no sarcasm—just pure disgust.

"Don't screw this up." Kevin smacked his visor shut and shot out of the garage.

Wolfgang dropped the bike into first gear and raced to follow.

[5]

Wolfgang couldn't think of a better way to explore Paris than astride the Triumph. The motor was powerful, if not oversized, providing plenty of juice to launch him between the lines of stalled cars filling the streets along his path to the highway.

Kevin drove like a brute, apparently deciding to overcompensate for his previous timidity. He gunned the bike at random and charged ahead at every available opening, but still lacked the skill to effectively navigate the traffic. Wolfgang quickly overtook him and was the first to slide down the ramp and onto France's A1 highway, stretching southwest toward the city.

Raven's cab driver was good. He'd already circumvented the bulk of the congested traffic and led Wolfgang by almost a kilometer. Wolfgang gunned the motor and swerved around a line of trucks laden with fresh produce. The food's fragrant odor mixed with the stench of petrol fumes and tire smog, but it wasn't an unpleasant smell. It smelled like adventure. Like something new.

Wolfgang held back a grin and whipped the bike between two cabs, lane splitting and gaining another two hundred meters on Raven's cab.

"Charlie Three, ease the hell up!" Edric barked over the radio. "You're drawing attention."

Wolfgang reluctantly relaxed on the throttle and glanced in his mirror. Kevin was a half klick back, riding easily behind the produce trucks with a clear view of Wolfgang.

He snitched on me. That rat.

Wolfgang rolled his eyes, then forgot about Kevin as Megan appeared a moment later, gently swerving between cars with the ease and grace of somebody who was accustomed to riding a bike. Her scarlet hair rode the wind over her shoulder blades, snapping against a denim jacket. She leaned close to the handlebars, her legs bent at the knee to mold her body next to the bike.

"Charlie Three, heads up!" Lyle said.

Wolfgang snapped his gaze away from the rearview mirror just in time to slam on the brake and swerve around the rear bumper of a bus stopped in the highway. His heart lurched toward his throat, and he hit the clutch, downshifting and twisting the throttle just in time to avoid being flattened by a horn-blaring truck behind him.

"Dammit, Charlie Three," Edric said. "What the hell are you doing?"

Wolfgang panted, feeling suddenly like crawling under a rock.

"Are you watching me?" he demanded.

Lyle's laugh was dry but still the most emotion Wolfgang had witnessed him express. "Why do you think they call me Charlie Eye? I've got you on satellite, Charlie Three."

Great.

Wolfgang flipped his visor up and sucked down a breath of smoggy air. He glanced to his left to see Megan riding with one hand on her hip, glaring at him from behind her visor. Then she turned away and rocketed ahead.

Wolfgang felt a rock in his stomach and smacked his visor shut.

Raven led them straight into the heart of Paris, circling the north section of downtown before his cab left the highway, and the three operators followed. The traffic began to slow, and Wolfgang looked up to see the sun break over the Arc de Triomphe directly ahead. Napoleon's Arch rose in majestic glory, dominating the center of a roundabout as the orderly highway became a hurricane of honking cars and squealing tires. At any other time, Wolfgang would have pulled off the road to admire the national landmark, but after almost kissing the backside of a bus, he forced himself to focus on the road and zipped right around it.

"Raven is two klicks ahead," Megan reported. "Charlie Two, Charlie Three, close ranks."

Wolfgang swerved amongst the slower-moving cars, drawing closer to Megan but still keeping her a few cars away. He was aware of Kevin on his left side but resisted the urge to look.

"I have Raven's cab stopping at the intersection of Saint-Germain and Rue Bonaparte," Megan said. "Intel, Charlie Eye?"

Wolfgang ran his tongue over dry lips as he felt the thrill of impending action wash over his mind. Be it Paris or Cleveland, at the end of the day, he was an operator. And he was about to operate.

"Confirmed, Charlie One," Lyle said. "I have him on satellite. Raven is exiting the cab and approaching Café Les Deux Magots."

"This could be it," Edric said. "Park the bikes and move in. Eyes on the street."

"Copy that, Charlie Lead. Moving in."

The highway rumbled beneath the tires of Wolfgang's bike as the buildings fell away and the road rose onto a bridge. Sunlight blazed down, warming his back and glistening off the glassy surface of the river Seine, stretching out to either side. Wolfgang stole a glance to his left and caught sight of France's famed Grand Palais, rising like a football stadium to the left of the highway. The structure's glass roof reflected the light back toward the water, and everything around him gleamed in pure gold.

The City of Lights . . . even in broad daylight.

Megan led the way past Grand Palais and back into the tangle of city streets. Five minutes later, Wolfgang's bike ground to a halt in a narrow parking space next to Megan's and Kevin's. He cut the motor and lifted his helmet. Megan and Kevin were already gone, splitting off in different directions as predetermined by Edric.

"Charlie Three, hurry it up," Edric snapped. "Eyes open!"

Wolfgang ran his hand through his hair to straighten it, then adjusted his jacket and hurried toward the café.

All around him, bustling Parisians collided with clueless tourists, laughing and shouting, pressing each other to the side and waving for cabs. In that respect, at least, Paris was no different than any big city. Lots of people crammed in a small place, all hurried and animated, and fully consumed by the human experience. Except that today, unbeknownst to the tourists and locals alike, one CIA agent, a team of armed operators, and maybe a couple of Russian assassins, were lost in the mix.

A police car rolled by, and Wolfgang resisted the urge to look at it. His stomach twisted, and he pressed his arm closer to his side, feeling the gun against his ribcage. What would happen if he were caught in Paris, armed and undocumented? Would Edric bail him out?

"Charlie Lead, I have a visual on Raven," Megan said, jarring Wolfgang back to the job at hand. "He's taken a seat inside the café, near a window."

"Copy that, Charlie One. Any sign of our Russian friends?"

"Negative. But I'm still fifty yards out."

"Move into the café and assume a surveillance position. Charlie Two, move one block down Saint-Germain. Charlie Three, take up surveillance opposite the café."

Wolfgang quickened his walk as the café appeared at the next street corner. The building was six stories tall, triangular in shape, and dressed in stunning French scrollwork, with the café built into the bottom floor. Tourists and Parisians crowded around the entrance, and every table visible on the other side of the glass was occupied.

"Shouldn't I remain close to the café?" Kevin barked across the comm. "Charlie Three can take distance. I need to be closer to the target—"

"Assume your assigned position, Charlie Two," Edric said.

Wolfgang saw Kevin fifty yards ahead, moving

away from the café. His posture radiated irritation, and the bigger man cast frequent glances over his shoulder.

That's why Edric wants you in the shadows. You're too obvious.

Wolfgang stepped onto the sidewalk, opposite the café, and shoved his hands in his pockets, pretending to admire the building's decorative stonework as he surveyed the block, one angle at a time.

"Charlie Three in position," he whispered.

"Charlie One in position."

Wolfgang glanced across the café's entrance, hoping to catch sight of Megan. He couldn't see her, and he briefly wondered how the hell she'd gotten inside the café at all. It was packed to the brim.

"Charlie Two?" Edric asked.

Kevin's voice was curt. "In position."

"Great. Eyes sharp, now," Edric said. "Any sign of Spider?"

All three of them radioed back in the negative, and for a while, the comms went silent. Wolfgang stood next to the curb amid the throng of pedestrians and surveyed the block, doing his best to look like just another tourist, starstruck by the Parisian fairy-tale around him.

Raven sat next to the window. Seeing him in person did little to alter Wolfgang's impressions of him based on the photograph. He was tall, with hair as black as night—hence the call sign, perhaps. Late forties, maybe early fifties, depending on how his genetic dice had fallen. Raven ordered a drink in a white china cup and sipped it while pretending to read a book. Wolfgang could tell by the angle of the man's face that he was reading the crowd outside the café rather than anything on the page.

Wolfgang switched his attention to the faces that passed along the sidewalk, searching for a Russian assassin. What did Russian assassins look like, anyway? Not like the movies, surely. Not dressed in black, with pale eyes and silenced pistols. No, these people would be professionals, trained to blend in, just like he was. And in this environment, crowded with noisy people and honking cars, it would be as easy for an assassin to vanish as it was for Wolfgang or for Spider.

Which means I'll never find them in this crowd.

Not only would he not find them, it would also be impossible to protect Spider if he took a seat with Raven directly in front of a window, fully exposed. Wolfgang needed to put himself in the shoes of an assassin. If he were here to kill Spider, and Spider was going to meet with Raven next to that window, where would he be?

Wolfgang's attention switched from the thronging crowds to the buildings that surrounded the café. The block was wide, with five streets intersecting together in a sort of knot, right in front of the building. On every corner were other buildings, apartments, and offices, with little shops and bakeries on the ground floors, all full of windows and facing the street. People churned in and out of those buildings, hailing cabs and shoving past each other as cars and buses whirred past.

The windows.

There were so many windows, but not all of them had an unobstructed view of Raven's position. Wolfgang squinted into the sun and scanned first one building, then the next, running his eyes along each floor, searching for irregularities.

Kevin's voice broke across the radio. "I have a target moving south along Saint-Germain! Matches Spider's description. Charlie Eye, do you have him?"

"Hold, Charlie Three . . ." Lyle said.

Wolfgang ignored the exchange and continued to scan the windows. His stomach tightened with an increasing unease—a practiced instinct he'd learned to follow over years of mishaps and near-death mistakes.

Their position was far too exposed. Raven's position was far too exposed. A lone sniper, nestled in an elevated position less than fifty yards from Raven's seat next to the window, wouldn't need a high-powered rifle. He could take both Raven and Spider out with two quick shots from a silenced .17 HMR, or even a high-powered air gun. There would be no sound—just two men crashing forward over a coffee table, with blood spraying from their skulls.

"I can't confirm identity. The satellite is lagging," Lyle said. "Charlie Two, can you confirm physical attributes?"

"He's short," Kevin said. "Five-seven, five-eight. Round glasses. European complexion. I can't determine any more without closing in. Should I proceed?"

"Negative, Charlie Two," Edric said. "Do not approach. Maintain cover."

Wolfgang shot a glance back up Saint-Germain. He saw the man immediately, working his way toward the café with a briefcase in one hand, the other hand jammed in his pocket. Was it Spider, or was it an assassin armed with a silenced pistol?

What would I do if I were the assassin?

Wolfgang chewed his lip, then turned back to the surrounding buildings. He wouldn't use a pistol. He wouldn't get that close.

"Working the satellite now. I think I have an image," Lyle whispered over the headset.

Wolfgang saw movement from the fourth floor of an apartment building across the street from the café. A Juliet balcony was mounted to the wall, directly in front of an open window. He could have sworn that window was closed only five seconds before. Now it was open, and while darkness shrouded the apartment's interior, he knew he'd seen something move.

"Charlie Lead," Wolfgang said, keeping his eyes fixed on the window. "I have movement. Fourth floor apartment building, across from the café."

"Monitor, Charlie Three. Hold position."

Wolfgang squinted into the sun. He would have held his hand up, shielding his eyes, but the gesture would draw attention. Instead, he ignored the discomfort and focused on the window.

There it was. Another movement. A shadow in the apartment.

"I have the image!" Lyle said. "Running facial recognition now. I think this is Spider."

"Where is he?" Megan asked from inside the café.

"One hundred yards from the café and closing," Kevin said.

"Stay on him, Charlie Two," Edric said.

Wolfgang pressed his finger against his ear, adjusting the earpiece. "Charlie Lead, I have movement in this apartment. Open window with clear line of sight to Spider's route."

"Hold your position until we confirm identity," Edric said.

Then Wolfgang saw it—a hard outline running perpendicular to the spindles of the Juliet balcony, pointed toward the café.

"Gun!" Wolfgang snapped. "I'm moving in!"

[6]

Wolfgang broke into a run, launching himself off the sidewalk and into the street as horns blared and Edric barked over the radio.

"Negative, Charlie Three! Hold your position. Do not engage!"

Wolfgang ignored the order, keeping one eye on the window as he ran. He could still see the outline of the rifle muzzle pointed at the café.

Tires shrieked, and Wolfgang twisted, his hip glancing off the front corner of a car as an irate motorist screamed at him in French. He jumped back onto the sidewalk and crashed toward the first door he saw, his breath whistling through his teeth as he smacked his elbow against the gun beneath his jacket. All his second thoughts about carrying the weapon were gone now. He was about to take down a

Russian sniper, right in the heart of a European city, and he was likely to need all the firepower he could get.

A glass door with a reception desk guarded the side entrance to the apartment complex. Wolfgang skidded past the desk and took the first hallway that led to the edge of the building. He instinctively knew that a stairwell would be located there, providing the most efficient method of escape in the event of a fire.

Edric continued to shout over the earpiece, but he wasn't shouting at Wolfgang any longer. The commands were directed at Kevin and Megan, ordering them to reposition to cover Wolfgang's vacancy.

"Target has stopped!" Kevin shouted. "He saw Charlie Three moving. He's backing away."

"Charlie Two, stay on him," Edric ordered. "Charlie One, stay with Raven!"

Wolfgang reached into his ear and dug the earpiece out, cramming it into his pocket as he bounded up the stairwell. He took the steps three at a time and launched himself around the corner of each landing. His heart pounded, and in his mind he counted the number of windows from the corner of the building to the window he'd seen overlooking the café. Was it six? Or seven? He wasn't sure, and it mattered.

He reached the fourth floor and slid to a halt, catching his breath and laying his hand gently on the door handle. Quiet, now. Not too fast. He didn't want that rifle redirected at him. The fourth-floor hallway was quiet and still. Each door, made of wood and painted in different shades of bright pastels, was shut and bolted, with glistening Roman numerals to mark the apartment number.

Wolfgang slid his hand beneath his jacket and felt the comforting weight of the Beretta. He closed his eyes momentarily and envisioned the window again. It was the seventh window from the corner; he was sure of it now. He *had* to be sure.

He opened his eyes and hurried down the hall, bending low and keeping the gun inside his jacket. He would try the knob first, and if it was unlocked, he would ease inside before drawing the gun.

The door was unlocked, and he held his breath as he pushed it open, mentally pleading for it not to squeak. The apartment on the other side was dark, quiet, and empty, with wooden floors that were polished but dusty. There was a kitchen on his right, and from someplace on the other side of the dining room, soft light drifted toward him. Light from the open window.

Wolfgang eased the handgun out of his jacket as he pressed the door shut and held his breath. He heard the distant blast of horns and a chorus of voices from the streets below. He could smell coffee in the air and pastries from the café. It was the smell of

Paris, and it shielded the scent of a Russian assassin in the room.

Wolfgang held the gun up, bracing his shooting hand and slipping into the dining room. It was empty also, but light spilled over the hardwood from the sitting room on the other side of the door. He drew a half breath through dry lips, then crouched and stepped into the next room. It was empty, like the rest. An open window looked over the Juliet balcony, with a white silk curtain flapping in the breeze. But on the floor were marks in the dust—twin scrapes about ten inches apart, just inside the window.

A rifle's bipod sat there. I was right.

Wolfgang took a cautious step forward, then glanced around the room. Nobody was visible, but there was only one entrance to the apartment. The Russian had to be inside. He had to be close. He had to be—

Wolfgang heard the soft creak of the hardwood only a millisecond before the first blow hit him between the shoulder blades like a baseball bat, sending him rocketing forward and crashing face-first onto the floor. The Beretta spun out of his hand, and he rolled over, kicking out with both legs for the shins of his attacker. His desperate attempts at defense were useless. The shadow of a man in all black encircled him with deft agility, moving toward his head. Wolfgang instinctively shielded his head with both arms as he tried to roll out of the way, but his attacker's movements were a ploy. The Russian stepped backward like a cat, landing on one foot and sending the other smashing into Wolfgang's stomach.

The air rushed from Wolfgang's lungs, and his arms flew toward his middle, bracing for another blow and leaving his head exposed. The butt of the rifle crashed toward his temple only a moment before his head erupted in pain and everything went black.

The Triumph's motor died with a gentle rumble, and Wolfgang deployed the kickstand but didn't dismount. He looked at the other two Triumphs parked twenty yards farther down the hotel parking lot, and then the white panel van parked next to the dumpster in the back.

Edric had booked them a two-room suite at the Hilton near the airport, which was large enough to provide a reliable safe house with multiple routes of approach. The team hadn't planned on using it. The plan was to be back in the air by now, popping champagne and collecting paychecks.

Wolfgang winced. His head pounded from the impact of the rifle butt on his temple, and it still hurt to breathe. But mostly, it hurt to be him, to be sitting there knowing he had to face the team.

They're going to blame me. Maybe they should.

Wolfgang slid off the bike, hung his helmet on

the handlebar, and walked into the hotel's lobby. He picked up his keycard at the main desk, using the fake passport Edric provided—John Altman, a Canadian businessman traveling for pleasure—and then took the elevator to the eighth floor. His stomach didn't churn anymore, but that was probably because the muscles were so bruised by the impact of the Russian's boot on his abdomen.

What was he thinking? He should have waited in the apartment's hallway or just inside the door. After all, where was the Russian going to go? He was boxed in.

Wolfgang stopped outside the suite and ran a hand through his hair. He wasn't sure if his face was bruised, but there was dirt all over his T-shirt, and his leather jacket was scratched. He looked like a fool.

Nothing for it.

He opened the door and was unsurprised to find the lights off. Two steps in, and he heard heavy footfalls coming toward him from the main room.

"You moron! You tryin' to get us all killed?"

Kevin barreled forward like a charging bulldog, his eyes blazing hatred. He grabbed Wolfgang by the collar and slammed him against the wall. "Are you working for the Russians?" Kevin snarled, his face only inches away.

Wolfgang snapped. He grabbed Kevin's elbow with one hand and shoved it inward, slicing Kevin's leverage in half before plowing his left knee into his groin. Wolfgang slid out of his grip, spinning him by the arm and driving him onto the floor. Wolfgang landed on his lower back, twisting Kevin's right arm toward his shoulder blades.

Kevin shouted, and Wolfgang drove the heel of his palm into his neck, shoving his face into the carpet and completely disabling him. "Don't you *ever* question my loyalty, you overgrown, arrogant piece of meat! I've met dogs who are smarter than you!"

Kevin wriggled and grunted in pain as Wolfgang applied more pressure to his arm, knowing he was only an inch away from snapping it. Then he felt powerful hands dig into his coat from behind, and before he could resist, he was slung to the left, farther down the hallway. Megan stood behind him, her eyes blazing. "Stop it, you idiots! Are you out of your minds? We've got work to do!"

Wolfgang lay on the floor, propped on one elbow. He shot his nemesis a sideways glare, then picked himself up and stumbled into the suite.

Edric stood next to the window, cradling a whiskey glass in his good hand and watching Wolfgang in stoic silence. Wolfgang avoided his gaze and crashed onto the nearest couch, wiping sweat from his forehead.

Kevin barreled in a moment later. His bottom lip bled from a cut, and he looked ready to commit murder. "He blew it!" Kevin shouted, spitting blood and saliva and pointing at Wolfgang. "We should never have brought him. He's a liability!"

"Get a drink, Kevin," Edric said. His voice was calm, but there was an edge of restrained anger just beneath the surface.

Kevin stumbled to the minibar and poured himself three shots of bourbon. Megan, with cheeks flushed, settled into a chair across from Wolfgang and dusted off her pants.

Edric turned to Wolfgang, took a sip of his drink, and cleared his throat. "What the hell happened, Wolf?"

"I told you. I saw a sniper on the fourth floor of the apartment building across from the café. He had a clear shot down Saint-Germain and of the window where Raven was sitting. I made a call."

"You made a call?" Kevin said. "Are you kidding me?" He slammed his glass down and barreled across the room, making it halfway before Megan shot her foot out. Kevin almost tripped, catching himself on the edge of a chair.

"Sit down, Kevin," Edric said. He turned back to Wolfgang. "What do you mean, you made a call?"

"The sniper was gonna have a clean shot if I didn't move in. It was a calculated risk, and I made a call. I moved in."

"Right. Only you're not *paid* to make calls, are you? *I'm* paid to make calls. You're paid to obey them."

"Come on, Edric." Wolfgang rolled his eyes. "You trained me to use my head."

"I did. But I also trained you to follow orders, and what you did today not only had the potential to blow the entire operation, it also endangered the lives of every person on this team. Have you considered that?"

"If I didn't move, he could've made the shot."

"I'm aware of that," Edric said, his tone boiling with growing tension. "Let me tell you what else I was aware of. I was aware that Lyle was having difficulties with the satellite but was only moments away from obtaining a clear image of the target. Do you know how valuable it would've been to confirm identity on Spider? We never got the chance because *you* spooked him before Lyle got the image."

"The Russian was gonna shoot."

"Probably not. Most likely he would have waited for Spider to sit down with Raven because the Russians aren't clear on this guy's identity, either. Even if he did plan to take Spider out on Saint-Germain, Kevin knew where the sniper was, which means he knew how much time we had before the Russian had a clear shot, and we *needed* that time to get the satellite working. You didn't know that because it's not your job to know that. It's my job."

Wolfgang swallowed and glanced around the room. He noticed Lyle for the first time. The wiz sat in the far corner behind the lunch table, nestled behind computers. His beady eyes overlooked a laptop screen, watching Wolfgang.

Wolfgang looked away. "You're right," he mumbled. "I was out of line. I'm sorry."

"Sorry," Kevin snarled. "Lot of good that does."

Edric turned to Kevin. "I'm not happy with you, either, hotshot. I told you to stay on Spider. Where is he?"

Kevin's gaze dropped to the floor, and his cheeks flushed.

"You lost him," Edric said. "So now Spider is gone, the Russians know what Wolfgang looks like, and the CIA is raising hell. This entire operation is teetering on the edge of collapse for one reason—this team failed to maintain discipline. I've never seen such a shit show in my life. We were all over the place!"

Edric's voice rose in intensity as he spoke, ripping through the room like a hail of bullets. Wolfgang winced and looked down at the floor. He wasn't angry or defensive anymore. He just felt like a fool.

Edric drained his glass and slammed it down on the counter. "Let me be clear. If any of you ever leave your post, or violate this or any future mission in any way, you're done. No excuses, no conversations. You'll never work for SPIRE again." Without another word, he stomped across the room and disappeared into a bedroom, slamming the door behind him.

[7]

The hours dragged by as the sun rose over Paris, then descended toward the ocean. Edric remained in his bedroom, leaving the four others to occupy themselves however they chose. Kevin drank until Megan cut him off, then he sat at the table next to Lyle and made a show of cleaning his firearms. He'd brought quite a few, and Wolfgang was impressed to see that they were already spotless.

Lyle remained behind the computer, still fussing with the satellite. It clearly bothered him that his technical issues had threatened the mission's success. He didn't speak to anyone but toiled at the computer for hours on end without moving.

Wolfgang rubbed his sore stomach and watched Megan. From his angle in the corner, he could see the bright flash of her eyes as she pored over maps of Paris and scratched notes on a pad. The sun that leaked between the blinds shone against her scarlet hair, turning golden over smooth skin. All the distance and weariness he'd noticed when they first met was gone. She worked with an intensity and a focus that would rival a professional scientist, ignoring the world around her as completely as Lyle.

He looked down at his battered hands. The Russian in the apartment had left Wolfgang's Beretta, and Wolfgang recovered it before returning to the hotel. It now rode in the shoulder holster again, but when he had crashed to the floor, his knuckles, propelled by the heavy gun, slammed into the hardwood.

I failed the team. I failed Edric. I failed Megan.

Wolfgang shoved his hands into his pockets and stood up, shuffling toward Megan. He could feel Kevin's stormy glower on him the entire way.

Wolfgang cleared his throat. "Hey, Megan?"

"What?" she said.

"I just . . . I just wanted to say I'm sorry about today."

"You should be." Her tone remained cold and uninviting.

Wolfgang sat in the chair next to her and dusted off his knees. "What are you working on?"

She turned back to the maps. With practiced twists of her elegant fingers, she left another line of neat handwriting on the pad. It was feminine and strong, written with confidence and command.

"Listen," he said. "I know I messed up today. There's no excuse. But you can count on me, all right? I really am good at my job, and I can contribute, too. Maybe if we talked more ahead of time, I could really add to the discussion and be an asset."

"An asset?" Megan's lips were set in hard lines, but he saw a vein flex in her temple. "I don't need an asset, Wolfgang. I need somebody who follows orders. We're not a family. We're not friends. We're a team, and all I need from you is for you to get the job done. Are we clear on that?"

Wolfgang felt like he'd been kicked in the gut again. He winced, feeling his cheeks flush. Megan looked back at her maps, and Wolfgang stood up, catching sight of Kevin smirking at him from the corner.

Is she always this cold?

Wolfgang found his way to the minibar and sifted through the alcohol until he found an unopened can of seltzer. It was warm, but the carbonation still helped to clear his throat. He felt Kevin's glare on him, and a bubbling wave of rage began to boil inside of him again.

What the heck is wrong with this guy? I've not done a thing to him.

Wolfgang turned to Kevin, ready to resolve the

issue head-on, but the bedroom door swung open, and Edric appeared, a notebook in one hand. "Gather up! We've got another shot at Spider." He flipped the overhead lights on and motioned everybody to the table. "Megan, bring the maps."

The group crowded around the table as Lyle reluctantly shifted his computers to one side. Megan spread out the map, and Edric traced it with the tip of a pen. He stopped at a point in the heart of Paris, just northeast of the Arc de Triomphe.

"The Hôtel Salomon de Rothschild. An exclusive, invite-only art gala is taking place there later tonight. Spider has reached out to Raven and rescheduled their meeting for during the event."

"So, he hasn't gone to ground," Megan said.

Edric let out a tired sigh. "Thankfully, no. He must've seen Wolfgang running, and it rattled him enough to cancel the rendezvous, but apparently, he's willing to reschedule."

"Not only that," Megan said, "he gave Raven the rendezvous point hours ahead of time. He wouldn't before."

"That's true," Edric said, "and it gives us more time to plan. But we have to assume that the Russians have obtained the same intelligence, and they also have time to prepare. They still want this guy dead, and we can only assume they're willing to shoot up a gala to get the job done."

"So, what's the play?" Kevin said. "Do we establish a perimeter and monitor for intruders?"

Edric shook his head. "No. Spider chose the gala as a rendezvous because he believes it'll be safe. I can only assume that hotel security is already pretty tight, and like I mentioned, it's an invitation-only party. Spider provided Raven with a fake invite. They will each enter the party posing as VIPs, and I'm sure the Russians will do the same, which means . . ." Edric looked at Megan.

She began shaking her head almost immediately. "No. I told you, I don't play dress-up."

Edric smiled disarmingly. "Come on, Megan. I wouldn't ask if I didn't really need it. Raven provided a copy of the invite so we can doctor and duplicate it for you and an escort. Then Lyle can hack the hotel computer systems and add your pseudonyms to the electronic guest list."

"I told you, I'm not a Barbie doll. We can infiltrate the hotel via the roof and provide protection from the shadows. Armed."

"No go," Edric said. "That drastically increases the complexity of the mission. Megan, I need this. I need you to play ball."

Megan scowled but nodded once.

"Thank you." Edric turned back to the map. "Lyle and I will park the van two blocks away. We'll provide central control, and hopefully, satellite surveillance."

Lyle nodded quickly. "I've almost regained access. Shouldn't be a problem."

Wolfgang held up a hand. "Wait. *Regained* access? Does that mean what I think it means?"

Edric waved the comment off, but Lyle blushed. "Look, it's not like we can afford our own satellite."

"So, when you said earlier that you were having trouble with the satellite, what you meant was . . ."

"I was kicked off, yes. But no worries. I've just about hacked my way back in. We'll be good to go."

Edric waved his hand again. "Let Lyle take care of the satellite. Wolfgang, you've got other things to worry about. What's your tux size?"

"Wait, you're sending *him*?" Kevin lurched out of his chair, his fists balled. "He's an incompetent moron!"

"Sit down, Kevin." Edric snapped his fingers, but Kevin didn't budge.

"I don't like it, boss. I should go. Megan and I have worked together for years. We know each other!"

"You're right," Megan said. "And we both know you have the acting skills of a pop star on cameo. You'll blow our cover before we make it past the front door."

Kevin fumed. "Are you serious? Meg, come on. We did the London job together."

"It was a corporate board meeting, and you

played my bodyguard. Completely different scenario."

"You don't trust me."

"It's not about trust, Kevin. It's about skill set. Don't make this personal."

Kevin folded his arms. "James trusted me."

The room fell deathly silent, and Wolfgang noticed Lyle's gaze drop to the floor as darkness crossed Megan's eyes.

Edric spoke between gritted teeth. "Sit down, Kevin."

Kevin slumped into his chair, his cheeks dark red.

Megan turned away, facing the wall.

"I'm sorry," Kevin said. "I shouldn't have said that."

Wolfgang opened his mouth, but then thought better of saying anything. A hundred questions boiled into his mind, but this didn't seem like the right time to ask them or press an advantage over Kevin.

"Meg?" Edric said.

She turned around. "What's my identity?"

"Rebecca and Paul Listener, from Toronto." Edric produced a pair of fake Canadian passports from his coat and passed them to Wolfgang and Megan. "You've been married for three years. Paul teaches humanities at Centennial College, and Rebecca is a full-time art critic. You're traveling to

Paris on vacation, and your invite was courtesy of a friend in the art world. Be vague about that."

Wolfgang admired the passport, feeling the smooth perfection of the laminated pages, and tilted the primary ID page in the light to examine the inlaid Canadian seal. The passport was a perfect fake—or very close to it.

"The mission is simple," Edric said. "Kevin will drive you in and remain on standby for exfiltration, and if it comes to it, additional firepower. Once you're inside the gala, make your way around the party until you locate Raven. Stay with him until he meets with Spider. Wolfgang, we'll need a full facial image. Use the watch."

Wolfgang nodded. "What about the Russians?"

"Protecting Spider is still our primary objective—at least until he completes his rendezvous with Raven. After that, the CIA has requested we forestall any sort of fireworks until Raven has left Paris. Remember, they're looking for plausible deniability here. So, ideally, we'll shield Spider until the end of the gala. Then we'll withdraw, and what happens, happens."

"What about Wolfgang?" Kevin asked. His voice was still sulky but less hostile. "The Russians will recognize him."

Edric nodded. "Unfortunately, that's true. Wolfgang, were you able to identify the sniper?"

Wolfgang shook his head. There was no point in lying about it. "No, I never saw his face."

"Okay. In that case, he'll identify you before you identify him. That's not ideal, but it could put the Russians on guard. They know you aren't actually a humanities professor, but it's not like they'll set off any alarms. After all, they're working under false identities, also. The most important thing is for you to pick them out as soon as possible. Feed Lyle as many facial images as you can, and look out for the usual signals—body language, people who look out of place, people who are checking out faces more than they're checking out paintings."

"No problem," Wolfgang said. "What happens after I find them?"

"Hopefully, nothing. Stay between them and Spider, and stall for time. As soon as Raven and Spider complete their rendezvous, Raven will leave, and Spider probably will, also."

"What if the Russians . . . you know . . ." Wolfgang trailed off, unsure if he was playing up a movie stereotype.

"Go full Ivan and light the place up?" Edric leaned against the wall, rubbing his chin with one hand. "There's not a lot we can do about that. Kevin will be on standby in case you need additional muscle. If you're confident the Russians are about to turn up the heat, I guess I'd rather you disable them. Quietly, of course."

Wolfgang exchanged a glance with Megan. "I understand."

The room was silent for a minute as Kevin's brooding darkness hung over them like a black cloud. Wolfgang knew they were all thinking the same thing.

He cleared his throat. "Look, I screwed up today. I realize you guys are taking a risk by working with somebody you don't know. And I just want to say . . . I've got your backs. You can trust me."

There was a hint of a smile on Edric's face, too vague to call, but it still gave Wolfgang some reassurance.

"Everything that happened this morning is behind us," Edric said. "We move as a team, now. Charlie gets it done."

Megan grunted. "Charlie gets it done, but Charlie's gonna need shopping money."

[8]

Wolfgang stood in the main sitting room of the hotel suite and fidgeted with his cuff links. Following the brief, Megan had left the hotel and returned two hours later with a couple of shopping bags and two shoeboxes. She produced a brand-new tux from one bag, complete with a black bow tie, a pressed shirt, and silver cuff links. Wolfgang wasn't sure if a professor from a liberal arts college would wear cuff links, but he wasn't about to question her.

Megan disappeared into one bedroom, and Wolfgang dressed. Kevin left to rent a car that could pass as a private taxi, and Edric took a shower. Wolfgang wondered how you showered with a full-arm cast, and decided he probably didn't want to know.

"How do I look?"

Wolfgang turned to Lyle, flexing his arms and

wiggling his shoulders beneath the jacket. Lyle looked over his computer screen, squinting through his smudged glasses. Then, to Wolfgang's surprise, he stood up and stepped around the table, approaching Wolfgang and inspecting him from head to toe.

The tux fit well. It wasn't a custom garment by any stretch, but Wolfgang felt good in it. He just wished it left room for his gun. There was no chance of squeezing the Beretta into the confines of the form-fitting jacket, and he felt a little naked.

Lyle nodded once, then reached up and adjusted Wolfgang's bow tie. "Almost good enough," Lyle said.

"Good enough?" Wolfgang laughed. "Good enough for what?"

Lyle pointed toward the bedroom as the door clicked open. "To stand next to her."

Wolfgang turned, and the breath caught in his throat. Megan wore a jet-black evening gown, long enough to trail the floor, with a slit that ran up her right leg to just inches below her waist. The gown hugged her hips and was suspended by a single shoulder strap that rode just to the left of her neck.

Her hair was pinned back on one side, while the majority of her locks flowed loosely over her shoulders and down her exposed back. Her crimson lipstick matched her hair in a darker shade of red, but the whole ensemble was offset by an awkwardness in her posture that Wolfgang hadn't seen before.

Wolfgang swallowed, and Lyle laughed.

"What?" Megan snapped, avoiding his gaze.

"Nothing," Wolfgang mumbled. "You . . . you look nice."

"Great. Are you ready?"

Kevin acquired a black Mercedes sedan to ferry them to the gala. He drove without a word, chewing gum and glancing from time to time into the rearview mirror.

Wolfgang ignored him, sinking into the back seat and watching Paris flash by. The city was alive now, with lights within each building glimmering like a million stars as the Mercedes bounced through the streets and whizzed down the highway.

As they topped a hill and turned south toward downtown, Megan tapped on her window. "Look."

Wolfgang leaned over, peering through the glass. In the distance, he made out the elegant, curving outline of the Eiffel Tower, shooting up from the Parisian skyline like a giant in the night. It was so much taller than he expected, framed against the black skyline with just a couple of marker lights.

"Have you ever been?" he asked.

"I've been someplace a lot like it, once," Megan said, her voice a little wistful. "Never here. I thought it was usually illuminated at night."

"Maintenance," Wolfgang said. "I read about it in a travel brochure."

Megan said nothing, and Wolfgang sat back, his focus drawn away from the distant tower and back to her legs, crossed over each other with casual elegance. She leaned back and closed her eyes, and for a moment, Wolfgang just stared. He was conscious of Kevin glaring at him through the rearview mirror, but he didn't care.

Screw this guy. I'm done worrying about him.

After another ten minutes, Kevin turned onto a quiet street, and Wolfgang saw other cars lined along it: Mercedes, Bentleys, Rolls-Royces, and a smattering of supercars purred in neat lines, all gently circling through the hotel's main entrance. Wolfgang leaned close to the window, admiring the display of opulence and wealth, his attention settling on a bright-red Ferrari with gloss-black wheels. Wolfgang knew very little about cars beyond basic brands, but this car was beautiful in every sense of the word, hugging the ground and rumbling with the restrained power of its massive Italian engine.

Wolfgang pictured himself behind the wheel of a car like that, rocketing up the California coast. He imagined riding with the windows down, the radio playing, and somebody special sitting next to him.

Focus, fool. You don't have time for this.

Wolfgang shelved the daydream and turned his attention to the people gathered around the cars. A small crowd of men in tuxedos and women in evening gowns stood in knots, laughing and migrating inside.

Megan pressed her earpiece into her right ear, then turned to Wolfgang. "Got yours?"

Wolfgang nodded, slipping the earpiece out of his pocket and into his ear.

"Keep it in your ear this time," she said.

A valet approached Megan's door, bowing and opening it in one smooth motion. In a flash, Megan's icy expression melted, replaced by a smile both warm and austere. Wolfgang felt his heart lurch, and he hesitated a moment in the car, watching her walk.

"If she gets hurt," Kevin said, "I'll kill you."

Wolfgang cocked his head, almost willing to let the threat go, then he smacked Kevin on the arm. "Kev, you couldn't kill me if I was tied to an electric chair. Keep the motor warm, will you?" He slid out of the car, adjusting his tie.

Megan waited at the bottom of the steps, glancing back at him. To his surprise, she reached out for his arm, and he accepted while trying to disguise his satisfaction.

Act or no act, it still felt great for her not to be glaring daggers at everybody.

They ascended the red-carpet stairs, arriving at the admissions guard at the top.

"Mr. and Mrs. Listener, Toronto," Wolfgang said.

The guard smiled and bobbed his head, then checked his iPad.

Wolfgang stiffened a moment, suddenly realizing he'd never received confirmation from Lyle that the hack was successful.

"Welcome to the gala, monsieur, madame."

The guard nodded them in, and Wolfgang relaxed a little. So far, so good.

"Charlie Lead, all systems, check."

"Charlie Eye, I'm live. Satellite is back online."

"Charlie One, we're in."

"Charlie Two, on standby."

Wolfgang started to speak, but Megan just shook her head. "Relax, hot stuff," she said. "You're as tense as Kevin."

Wolfgang flushed, following Megan through the hotel's double doors and into a stunning lobby. Bright lights glistened from chandeliers, reflecting off marble flagstone flooring and illuminating rows of oil paintings that lined every side of the lobby and proceeded into the halls. Everywhere, people in expensive evening attire gathered, admiring paintings and murmuring as they sipped champagne. White-gloved servers scurried in and out of the main lobby, replacing champagne flutes and serving hors d'oeuvres.

"Just like the movies," Wolfgang whispered.

Megan rolled her eyes. "Why do you think I didn't want to come?"

"I'm not sure, actually. I was wondering about that."

Megan shot a sunbeam smile at a server bright enough to blind him, and accepted a champagne flute.

Wolfgang waved the server off with a polite smile.

"You should drink," Megan said. "You'll stick out if you don't."

"I don't drink alcohol."

"Why the hell not? Are you sober?"

They drifted closer to a row of paintings as Wolfgang scanned the room for any sign of Raven. The American was nowhere to be seen.

"I'm not sober. I just don't drink. Why didn't you want to come to the party?"

They settled in front of an obscure art piece that may have depicted a battle, or a sunrise, or a circus—Wolfgang really had no idea—and continued to scan the room.

"Let's just say I'm not much for tropes," Megan said.

"Tropes?"

"You know. The hot spy girl dressing up for a party to catch the bad guys."

"So, you admit to being hot. I'm relieved. I was starting to think I was seeing visions."

Megan stared at him a moment, and he almost thought she'd slap him. A smirk played at the corner of her mouth, and she took a sip of her champagne, leaving a lipstick smudge on the flute. "That's *almost* funny."

"Kind of my move," Wolfgang said with a self-deprecating shrug. "Why don't you like tropes?"

"Hypothetically?"

"If you like."

"Okay. Hypothetically, dressing up like this makes me feel a touch objectified."

"Hmm. I can respect that. But can I offer an alternative interpretation?"

Megan pretended to study the painting and took another sip of her champagne, and Wolfgang took her silence as permission to proceed.

"Everybody on the team respects you. Kevin waits on you like a freaking lap dog. You're the only person whose opinion Edric blindly accepts. You've got me ready to jump off a building, if that's your call."

Megan rotated the flute in her fingers. "Your point?"

Wolfgang shrugged. "Doesn't sound much like objectification to me. Sounds more like . . . a pedestal."

Megan lifted one eyebrow, and he thought he saw that smirk playing at her lips again. She finished the champagne and turned away. Wolfgang followed her, casting casual looks at the passing art and settling on a painting that was most definitely a nude of some kind of princess. He twisted his arm until his watch camera captured the canvas, and Lyle uttered an involuntary snicker over the earpiece.

Megan jabbed him in the ribs. "You're a child. Focus on your job for a change."

A sudden rustle from the crowd brought a stillness to the room, and then everybody started moving toward another set of double doors at the end of the hallway. Wolfgang and Megan moved with them, checking every face they passed. There were lots of old, overweight men in tuxedos—one of whom actually wore a monocle—but no sign of the trim, dark Raven. Wolfgang felt uneasy again. In this crowd, it shouldn't have been hard to spot the Russians. He needed only to look for men who weren't twenty pounds overweight and guzzling booze. But that also meant there would be no confusion for the Russians in identifying Raven, or Spider, or himself, for that matter.

"Sitrep," Edric said.

"We're moving into the ballroom," Megan said. "I think there's gonna be a speech."

They passed through the double doors and into a massive square room. More appetizers lined one wall, while a string quartet in the corner sat stiff and upright on their stools. The center of the room was left open.

Wolfgang felt a twist in his stomach. *Dancing.* He didn't dance. In fact, he'd never danced, unless you counted a quick movement of the feet to dodge a bullet. Wasn't this supposed to be an art gala?

There shouldn't be dancing.

A soft clinking sound rang off a champagne flute, and the crowd grew quiet. Then a short man with tiny glasses and a bald head appeared at the front of the room, standing on a low platform. He held a mic, smiled, and then launched into a quick salutation in French. Wolfgang couldn't understand a word of it.

Megan stood attentively, appearing to watch the speaker while her eyes darted almost imperceptibly, scanning the room. Wolfgang followed suit but still didn't see Raven.

Raven should be here by now.

The speaker concluded his monologue with a clap of his hands and a big smile, and then the quartet began to play. Everybody in the room turned to their partner and, almost in unison, started dancing.

Megan sighed, then twisted and offered her hand with the enthusiasm of a janitor approaching a soiled toilet.

"I can't dance," Wolfgang mouthed, feeling his face flush.

"What's that? You can't dance?" Megan was loud enough for at least a few people standing nearby to hear, not to mention the entire team.

Wolfgang's blush deepened, and Megan offered

a slight smirk. "Relax, dude. Just follow me, and don't step on my feet."

He took her hand reluctantly, and they swung into a smooth side-step, followed by a turn, then a backstop. Wolfgang struggled to keep up, even though Megan moved decidedly slower than the rest of the crowd. His face flushed again, and Megan actually laughed. It was a dull sound, but it still brought to life that warmth in his chest again.

"Relax," she said. "Pull me a little closer . . . that's it. Now, move like the wind. Smooth . . . easy. Feel the music."

Wolfgang did feel the music. He focused on the violin's gentle hum, matched by the deep throb of the upright bass and the rich gravity of the cellos. The beautiful, haunting sound made him momentarily forget about the mission, and he lost himself in the reality of where he was standing. In Paris, the City of Lights, the city of love, dancing with a beautiful woman at a beautiful gala.

Her grey eyes flashed fire as she ducked and twisted, challenging his ability to keep up. Wolfgang was certain he looked like a waddling duck next to the rich and accomplished art connoisseurs around him, but he didn't care anymore. He pretended he knew what he was doing, and it seemed to help.

The music wound down, and they stopped. Wolfgang wobbled on his feet a minute, suddenly feeling a little dizzy. He steadied himself and offered his best imitation of the bows the men around him performed.

"You're pretty good," he said.

Megan released him and stepped back. To his surprise, she offered another smile—softer this time.

"You're not half-bad yourself."

She led him to the edge of the room and selected two flutes of champagne from a server. She passed him one and held up hers. "You don't have to drink, but at least pretend."

Wolfgang returned her smile and lifted the flute, but Megan's gaze darted over his shoulder to the far side of the room.

"Charlie Lead, I have eyes on Raven."

Wolfgang started to turn, but Megan stopped him.

"Don't look now. You'll draw attention. He's in the corner, near the hors d'oeuvres."

"Charlie One, close on target," Edric said. "Charlie Three, maintain surveillance."

Megan drained her flute and set it down, then set off casually across the room without a second glance at Wolfgang. He felt a tug of longing watching her go, but he shrank back against the wall and scanned the room until he saw Raven.

The American stood alone in the corner, dressed in a white tux, sipping champagne. The string quartet had started up again, but nobody danced. The crowd milled about, enjoying the food and drifting in and out of the art galleries. Raven seemed to ignore them all, but to Wolfgang's trained eye, the American was looking for something. Or someone.

"No sign of Spider," Wolfgang whispered. "Charlie Two, do you see anything outside?"

The line remained silent.

Wolfgang licked his lips and scanned the room again. "Charlie Two, anything from outside?"

Still, Kevin said nothing. Then Wolfgang felt a powerful hand descend on his arm from behind and yank him into the hallway.

[9]

Wolfgang slid backward into the shadows before he could reach for the pistol that wasn't even there. He grunted and felt his shoulder blades collide with the wall as his attacker stepped in front of him. Wolfgang braced his knee for a groin shot and twisted to break free of the hold, then he looked up and faced his attacker for the first time.

Kevin shoved a meaty hand against Wolfgang's throat, half choking him while his free hand descended over Wolfgang's ear, cutting off the mic built into the earpiece.

"What the hell are you doing?" Kevin snarled.

Wolfgang wheezed and tried to break free, but Kevin owned all the leverage. His forearm pinned Wolfgang's neck against the wall, held just beneath his chin, while Kevin continued to block off the earpiece.

Wolfgang choked and tried to kick. Kevin blocked the attack and then drove the toe of his shoe into Wolfgang's shin. Pain shot up Wolfgang's leg and his eyes watered. He gasped for breath, and Kevin leaned closer.

"You greasy weasel!" Kevin snarled. "You think I'm gonna let you poach Meg like this?"

Wolfgang's vision blurred, and Kevin relaxed his forearm just a little. Precious oxygen flowed in, and Wolfgang gasped it down. "What's wrong with you?" His voice sounded distorted in his own head with Kevin's palm still clamped over his ear.

"I'm watching you, you rat. Back off. She's not a piece of meat!"

Wolfgang gritted his teeth and smacked Kevin's hand away from his ear. Then he dug out the earpiece and flicked the power switch off.

"You wanna do this? Right here and now? I'll *wreck* you." He stepped forward, his fists balling up, ready to fight. Then he caught sight of something out of the corner of his eye and turned to see a couple walking across the ballroom, approaching the hallway. He relaxed his shoulders and stepped back. The couple passed by, casting each of them a suspicious glance but saying nothing.

As soon as they rounded the corner, Kevin closed the distance. "I'll make this perfectly clear, shithead.

Meg is off the market. So back off. I'll kill you, and I won't think twice about it. It wouldn't be the first time."

There was an edge in Kevin's voice that chilled Wolfgang to the bone. He saw a blend of self-righteous justification and stupidity in his dark eyes—perhaps the most dangerous cocktail known to man.

Wolfgang's blood boiled, but he rubbed his throat and slid the earpiece back into his ear. "We've got work to do," he snarled. "But don't worry. This isn't over."

Wolfgang flicked the earpiece on and was immediately flooded with radio chatter.

"Charlie Three! Do you copy? Target inbound, possibly Spider!"

Wolfgang hurried back into the ballroom, smoothing out the wrinkles in his jacket. He caught sight of Megan almost immediately, standing near the wall, her body tense and ready for action. He followed her line of sight to a clean-cut man in a tuxedo and black-rimmed glasses. Wolfgang walked with grace and purpose, making a beeline for Raven, who now stood near an emergency exit door.

"That's him," Kevin whispered from just behind Wolfgang. "That's the guy I saw at the café."

"Charlie Two, is that you?" Edric said.

Wolfgang and Kevin exchanged a glance, and Wolfgang saw the defeat in Kevin's eyes. He'd been caught away from his post. Wolfgang wanted to smirk, but he didn't have time.

"Charlie Eye, can you confirm identity of target?" Wolfgang twisted his left arm, aligning his watch's camera with Spider. He tracked Spider for ten feet, then dropped his arm to avoid drawing attention.

"Hold one, Charlie Three," Lyle said.

Wolfgang held his breath, counting the seconds as Spider drew closer to Raven.

Lyle's excited voice broke over the comms. "Identity confirmed! Target is Ramone Ortez. He's a Spanish-born physicist specializing in nuclear technology, currently employed by a conglomerate of nuclear power plant owners based in Kiev. No living family or known associates."

Nuclear technology. The blood chilled in Wolfgang's veins. He remembered Edric's briefing back in St. Louis when Edric mentioned that the CIA was attempting to mine information out of Spider about an impending attack. A *nuclear* attack. Was Spider building a bomb?

"Copy that," Edric said. "All right, everybody. This is it. We've got to give Raven time to obtain Spider's plan. Charlie One, close on Raven, but remain undercover. Charlie Two, where the hell are you?"

Wolfgang saw Kevin swallow and heard Edric's

threat echo in his mind: "*If any of you ever leave your post . . . you're done.*"

Kevin spoke clearly, without hesitation. "I'm with Charlie Three, Charlie Lead."

The line was silent for a moment, and when Edric spoke, his anger was barely contained. "Copy that. Establish a security perimeter. Any sign of our Russian friends?"

"Negative," Kevin said, scanning the room. Then he paused. "Wait . . . I've got two men entering the room from the north. Black suits, dark hair—"

Wolfgang held up his finger, then pivoted the watch toward the intruders, stepping into the room and searching over the tops of the guests' heads. Even though they wore matching tuxedos, nothing about them said 'art enthusiast,' but Wolfgang could smell 'Russian killer' from across the room.

"Hold on, Charlie Three," Lyle said again.

The seconds ticked past, and Wolfgang held the watch steady.

"I only got a clear image of one of them," Lyle said. "Facial recognition is coming up empty."

Just then, the left-hand man's gaze swept to the left side of the room and collided with Wolfgang's. He was a big man with long black hair and a dominant stance that reeked of military experience and a lifetime of giving orders. A split second passed, and then, like glass shattering on the floor, recognition passed across his face. A soft smirk tugged at his lips, and he lifted two fingers and tapped his temple.

Wolfgang recalled the impact of the rifle butt crashing through the air and colliding with the side of his head . . . right where the man tapped his fingers.

"That's them," Wolfgang snapped, lowering the watch and starting into the ballroom. "They're the Russians."

"How do you know?" Edric said.

"I know. One hundred percent."

"Copy that, Charlie Three. Keep them away from Raven. Watch out for guns. Charlie Two, take his flank."

Kevin stepped out behind Wolfgang, pivoting to the left and sliding his hand into his pocket as Wolfgang walked along the right-hand wall, circling toward the Russians and keeping his sights on them the entire time.

"Raven is on the move," Megan said. "He's approaching the gallery. Spider is with him."

"Stay on him, Charlie One!" Edric said. "Charlie Three, where are the bogies?"

Wolfgang said, "Moving toward the hallway, Charlie Lead. They've identified Spider."

"Copy that. Charlie One, stay in between Raven and the bogies. Charlie Two, Three—close in."

Kevin and Wolfgang quickened their stride, casting wary glances around the crowd of laughing, half-drunk art connoisseurs as they moved toward the main art gallery. The Russians were quicker, splitting up and taking separate hallways that both led to the gallery.

"Bogies have split," Kevin said. "They're closing in."

"Copy that. Stay on them."

Kevin and Wolfgang parted ways without a word, each taking the Russian closest to them as they moved into the hallways. Once more, Wolfgang was bitterly aware of the space beneath his arm where his pistol should have been. Why didn't he have a smaller gun? Or a knife? Or a freaking rock? Something.

The long-haired Russian with the devilish smirk led the way, walking in quiet confidence without glancing over his shoulder, even though he had to know Wolfgang was on his heels. It was Wolfgang's friend from the apartment outside the café.

You won't get me twice, Ivan.

Wolfgang quickened his stride, breaking into the main gallery and squinting under the bright lights. There was art everywhere, lining the walls and suspended on circular stands throughout the room. He caught sight of Raven disappearing down a short hallway and saw Megan stop short and cast an unwilling glance his way.

"Problem, Charlie Lead," Megan said. "Spider and Raven have entered the men's room. I can't follow without breaking cover."

Megan hesitated at the end of the short hallway, but Ivan didn't. He walked quickly across the room and right by her, winking as he passed.

"Move in, Charlie Three," Edric said. "Don't let him near Spider!"

Wolfgang broke into a fast walk, smiling quickly at an old woman he almost ran over on his way to the bathroom. Ivan shoved the bathroom door open and stomped inside like he owned the place, then Wolfgang heard a broken shout from Kevin over the radio.

"Charlie Lead! I'm engaged. Back alley!"

There was a crashing sound, then Kevin's muted scream.

"Charlie One, help him out!" Edric said.

"Copy that!" Megan broke into a run through the middle of the art gallery, breaking for the exit door to the back of the hotel.

"You're on your own, Charlie Three. Stay sharp!"

Wolfgang placed his palm against the bathroom door and shoved inside, ducking instinctively to avoid a surprise blow. But none came. The large bathroom had polished flagstone floor tiles and a line of marble sinks along one wall, with framed mirrors behind them. The door swung shut automatically as Wolfgang stepped inside, his shoes clapping against the flagstones.

Wolfgang crouched and saw Spider and Raven standing in the last stall near a fire exit barred with a red alarm latch. And then there was Ivan, standing at the sink and washing his hands under steaming water while watching Wolfgang in the mirror. Ivan grinned.

Wolfgang drew a slow breath and straightened his jacket. He glanced under the stalls again, but the men hadn't moved. If Raven and Spider were talking, he couldn't hear them. He turned back to Ivan and saw the big Russian's smile grow wider as he continued to rub his hands beneath the piping hot water.

Screw this guy.

Wolfgang stepped across the room, his shoes clicking like a tap dancer, and selected the sink two slots down. He flipped the water on and stared at his reflection in the mirror, keeping track of Ivan out of the corner of his eye.

"In Mother Russia, we treat bruises with vodka," Ivan said. He spoke softly enough that Spider and Raven wouldn't hear. His English was good, but heavily accented, like a true movie villain.

Wolfgang waited for the water to grow hot, then he ran his wet hands through his hair, finger-combing it into order and gently dodging the spot where Ivan's rifle butt had crashed into his head.

"Hell of a bruise you have, Amerikos," Ivan continued.

"It was a cheap shot," Wolfgang said without

taking his eyes off the mirror. "In the Land of the Free, we treat those with a beatdown."

"You haven't got the stones."

"I won't need stones for the likes of you, Ivan. You'll be eating through a straw when I'm finished with you."

Ivan pulled his hands from beneath the water and flipped the faucet off as his wolfish grin reflected toward Wolfgang in the mirror. Then he reached out without looking and tore a length of paper towel from the dispenser.

"Too bad we will never know," he said. "My comrade, Igor, is in alley dealing with your friends. When he is finished, he will join us. Then we will see how big your stones are . . . before we crush them."

"Why wait?" Wolfgang asked, turning the water off. "Let's get it on, right here, right now." He turned to face the bigger man.

Ivan's smile widened, but he didn't move.

"Oh, that's right. You can't," Wolfgang said. "You can't afford to make a scene. Not here. That's why you need Igor—so you can mop up the blood before the cops show up."

Fire flashed across Ivan's eyes, but he didn't say anything.

Wolfgang tore off a sheet of paper towel and stepped closer, glaring Ivan down as he dried his hands.

Then metal clicked against metal, and a hinge squeaked. Both Ivan and Wolfgang glanced impulsively toward the back of the room and saw Spider appear first. His face was white and sweat dripped down his cheeks as Raven walked just behind him.

Fear crossed Spider's eyes, and Raven appeared calculative as they both saw Wolfgang and Ivan. Moments ticked by in perfect stillness as all four men processed the situation, their minds spinning for the best move in this impossible, deadly game of chess.

Then Raven jumped. He grabbed Spider by his upper arm and spun, ramming his shoulder through the fire door and hurtling outside into the darkness. Only a second later, Ivan roared like a bear and lunged toward Wolfgang as a fire alarm screamed from overhead.

[10]

Wolfgang slipped to the left and stuck out his right foot just in time to dodge the charging Russian and trip him up. But Ivan caught Wolfgang by the arm, and they crashed to the floor in a tangled mess of flying legs and flipping coattails.

"Charlie Three, do you copy? What's going on?" Edric's shouts screamed through the earpiece, but Wolfgang didn't have a prayer of answering as he continued to roll.

Ivan landed on top, but before he could brace himself against the floor, Wolfgang delivered a rabbit punch to Ivan's jaw and spun to the right. The Russian's jaw crunched upward as teeth ground and splintered, then Ivan toppled. Wolfgang rammed his elbow against the floor, propelling himself up and on top, already preparing his next combo to Ivan's face.

Wolfgang's next punch landed squarely on Ivan's oversized nose, flesh meeting flesh, with bony, cartilage-crunching force. Blood spurted across Wolfgang's pressed white shirt, and he raised his fist again.

Ivan glared up with wild, crazy eyes, the grin having never left his face, and he spat blood at Wolfgang. "You punch like Polish bitch, Amerikos!" He bowed his back and rolled abruptly to the right. Wolfgang lost balance and hurtled backward, sliding across the floor and crashing into the first stall. His head snapped back against the polished marble of the stall wall with a dull crack, and his world spun. Ivan rolled to his knees, then jumped to his feet, his teeth dripping blood like a vampire as he hurtled forward.

Wolfgang was vaguely aware of the fire alarm still screaming overhead from the breached fire door, along with panicked voices and pounding feet outside the bathroom. Edric shouted in his ear again, but somehow, the only thing that mattered was the two-hundred-fifty-pound hunk of Siberia hurtling toward him like a pass rusher ready to sack the shit out of a panicking quarterback.

Wolfgang dipped to his right, ducking beneath the bottom edge of the stall wall, and then rolled under it only seconds before Ivan crashed into the marble at full force. Metal screeched, and a bracket tore loose. Wolfgang's head lay next to the toilet, barely shielded from the collapsing marble panel that crashed into the toilet. Porcelain shattered as water sprayed across his face and Ivan continued to roar.

Wolfgang felt a shoe slam into his exposed calf, then heard the sickening *click-click* of a pistol being chambered.

"Where are your stones?" Ivan shouted.

Two sharp pops cracked through the tight bathroom as a silenced pistol fired into the marble wall shielding Wolfgang. He rolled and crawled his way into the next stall as shards of porcelain and flakes of marble exploded behind him. Ivan directed his fire at Wolfgang's kicking legs, and Wolfgang felt a bullet tear through his pants, scraping his skin and barely missing his knee. He winced and jerked his leg inside the next stall as more gunshots rang out.

"This is Russian beatdown!" Ivan cackled, his feet pounding around to the front of the stalls.

Wolfgang's body was alive with adrenaline, his mind flooding with panic. He had to get to his feet. He had to find a weapon.

He rolled to his knees and slapped the lock on the stall door just in time to keep it closed under Ivan's next blow. The Russian swore, and Wolfgang danced backward as two bullets skipped and ricocheted beneath the stall wall.

"Dance, Amerikos! Dance, if you have the stones!"

Wolfgang stumbled backward. His heels hit the toilet, and he sat down with a crash as Ivan pressed the muzzle of his pistol against the crack in the stall door and blew the lock away.

"Now I put your head in toilet and make Russian hurricane!" Ivan plowed his shoulder against the door, and it burst open.

Wolfgang twisted, reaching to his right and lifting the lid off the toilet with both hands as Ivan slid inside, gun first.

The first bullet flew wide, smacking into the wall as Wolfgang ducked and swung with the lid. The leading edge of it crashed against Ivan's hands, hurling the gun aside as Wolfgang launched himself off the toilet. The gun clattered to the floor, and Ivan stumbled back. Wolfgang snatched the lid back, then twisted it and swung upward, piloting the corner of the lid straight into Ivan's nose.

Cartilage collapsed, and fresh blood sprayed from Ivan's face. He stumbled backward again, and Wolfgang pressed forward, driving him out of the stall and into the bathroom. Then Wolfgang delivered a lightning kick with his left shin, straight into Ivan's groin.

The big man grunted and fell forward onto his knees, unable to maintain his balance.

Wolfgang brought the lid down, full force across Ivan's skull, and said, "Where are your stones?"

The porcelain cracked as Ivan's eyes rolled backward, then the big Russian collapsed to the floor.

Wolfgang panted, dropping the lid's shattered

half and swabbing his bloody forehead with his sleeve.

Edric's voice was near panic. "Charlie Three! Do you copy?"

Wolfgang staggered to the sink and splashed water across his face. "I'm here, Charlie Lead . . . I'm here."

"What the hell is going on?"

"The Russian . . ." Wolfgang wiped water from his face. "He was confrontational."

"Not the Russian. Where's Spider?"

Wolfgang's heart lurched. *Spider*. He'd forgotten about him in the heat of the fight.

Wolfgang broke toward the fire door, pausing long enough to scoop up the Russian's fallen pistol. He wasn't sure how many rounds were left, but he wasn't about to crash through another door unarmed.

Biting night wind stung his eyes as he burst into the narrow street behind the hotel. The fire alarms faded behind him, but now he could hear the distant scream of European fire trucks hurtling toward the hotel. Voices shouted from the front of the building, but in the back, all was dark and still.

Wolfgang raised the pistol and turned down the street. It was framed on both sides by tall buildings that blocked out the streetlights and gave shelter to the dumpsters and heating units that lined either side of the road. Beneath the screech of the fire engines, the heaters hummed softly, masking Wolfgang's footfalls as he eased down the alley.

"I'm in pursuit," Wolfgang whispered.

He looked to the end of the alley, then behind him toward the hotel front. In truth, he had no idea which way to go or where to look. Spider could be anywhere by now. He could be halfway out of the city.

Wolfgang's stomach twisted in knots as he took another two steps into the alley. Maybe their mission was already accomplished. Raven had plenty of time to talk to Spider. Maybe he had already ascertained the date and location of Spider's planned attack, and maybe it didn't matter where Spider was anymore. He was the CIA's problem now.

But no. Something in Wolfgang's gut warned him that this wasn't over. Something was still wrong. Something felt cold and uneasy.

The sharpening breeze that whistled down the street bit through his tuxedo. He took another few steps into the alley and paused when something on the ground beyond the next dumpster caught his eye. He couldn't tell what it was, but by the soft angles and irregular shape, he knew it wasn't made of metal, and probably wasn't man-made at all.

Wolfgang broke into a jog, leading with the gun and closing on the object. His stomach churned as he heard Edric call through the earpiece again. Broken and distorted, his voice was becoming more difficult to discern, but Wolfgang wasn't listening anyway. He approached the dumpster from the back side and held the gun at eye level, then slowly turned the corner.

Spider lay on his back, staring skyward, his throat slit from ear to ear. Blood spilled across the pavement in a growing pool of rapidly cooling crimson. Wolfgang swept the gun left and right, but there was no sign of the killer, or of Raven.

Wolfgang stepped back. "Charlie Lead, I've located Spider. He's dead. Repeat, Spider is terminated."

Wolfgang's earpiece clicked and hissed.

Edric's reply sounded distant. "What is your location, Charlie Three?"

"Behind the hotel, in the street."

"Repeat, Charlie Three. You're breaking up." Edric's voice faded and clicked, then the earpiece beeped.

Wolfgang knelt next to the body, quickly digging through Spider's pockets, searching for anything useful. The pockets were empty, but as Wolfgang moved to search Spider's coat, another beeping filled his ears, this time not from the earpiece. It was from his watch.

He twisted his arm. The watch face blinked red, with a yellow message flashing in the middle of the screen: RADIATION DETECTED.

Wolfgang pulled his hand back, almost rolling

onto his ass, then looked down at the body again as he remembered Lyle's description of the watch. *"I call it a sniffer . . . It even has a built-in Geiger counter."*

Wolfgang pushed himself to his feet and took another step back as he scanned the length of Spider's body, from his slit throat all the way to his shoes.

His shoes. Wolfgang's gaze stopped on the exposed soles of Spider's dress shoes. They had leather soles, and the bottoms were stained with bronze-colored patches, from the heel to the toe. Wolfgang knelt down, leaning close to the shoes as the watch buzzed again. He reached out and scraped at the stains. Some of the substance lifted free of the soles in gummy strips. It was half-dried paint.

Wolfgang stood up again and took a step back, his mind racing.

A nuclear scientist, exposed to radiation, walking through paint . . .

The realization hit Wolfgang like a ton of bricks. He turned toward the alley and broke into a run, pressing his hand over his ear. "Edric! Edric, the attack is today! Here in Paris! There's a bomb in Paris!"

The earpiece remained quiet. Wolfgang pulled it out and tapped it against his leg, then jammed it in again and repeated his frantic monologue. Once more, he was answered only by silence, and a lead weight descended into his stomach as he remembered Lyle's other words about his gadgetry. *"The battery life isn't great."*

Wolfgang had neglected to charge the earpiece after the café mission. It was dead now—completely useless. He gritted his teeth and dashed around to the front of the hotel. People were everywhere, crowding around the firetrucks as firefighters dashed into the hotel, towing canvas hoses. Red lights flashed, and alarms screamed. Charlie Team was nowhere in sight.

Wolfgang pressed through the crowd, frantically searching the faces for Megan or Lyle, Edric, or hell, even Kevin.

Somebody. Now.

The breeze on his face intensified, bringing with it an omen of doom. He didn't have time to find the team. He was already out of time. His hands shook, and he scanned the parking lot. He needed a car. Something fast.

A low snarl echoed across the parking lot, and Wolfgang looked to his left. A knot of gala attendees had gathered around a substitute valet stand. They waited in line, shouting for their cars to be brought around as the wives shivered and the men cursed. The sound had come from the race-red Ferrari he'd seen earlier that night. The beast growled as it approached the valet stand, its lights flashing across the faces of the waiting gala attendees. Wolfgang broke into a run, shoving through the crowd as the driver's door of the Ferrari swung open and the valet stepped out. Wolfgang grabbed his arm and jerked him out of the way amid shouts from the crowd, then slid inside, slamming the door and hitting the locks. The valet snatched at the door handle, shouting at him to open it. Wolfgang ignored him and searched for the gear selector. There wasn't one, but there were three buttons built into the console next to his right leg: R, Auto, and LC—probably Launch Control.

Wolfgang hit the auto button and slammed on the gas.

[11]

People screamed, and the Ferrari roared. Wolfgang was hurled into the plush leather seat as the back wheels spun, and then the car launched out of the portico and hurtled toward the street.

Wolfgang slammed on the brakes and cut the wheel to the right, sliding around a corner in the parking lot before hitting the gas again and rocketing into the street. He couldn't hear the screaming pedestrians or fire engines now, only the bellow of the V12 engine filling his ears as the car hit redline and the dash lit up with a warning light. Wolfgang hit the paddle shifter, and the transmission clicked like a fine watch. The Ferrari blasted forward as if a rocket were launching him from behind. He swerved to dodge taxicabs and late-night buses as the blinding lights of Paris filled his view.

He turned to the dash and poked at the navigation screen next to the tachometer. Wolfgang saw what looked like a voice command button, and he smashed it.

"Take me to the Eiffel Tower!" he shouted.

"Bienvenue dans votre Ferrari. Veuillez dire une commande."

"I don't speak French! English!"

"Veuillez dire une commande."

Wolfgang looked up from the nav system just in time to pull the wheel to the right and slide into the roundabout surrounding Napoleon's Arch. Buses, cars, bicycles, and motorbikes surrounded him on all sides as people shouted and horns blared. He narrowly missed colliding with a taxicab as he completed a full circle of the arch, the Ferrari still roaring. A marker appeared on the nav screen, just a mile south of the arch on the other side of the river Seine. It was the Eiffel Tower.

Wolfgang turned back to the left, exiting his hectic orbit of the arch and shooting onto Avenue d'Iéna. Trees leaned over the street on both sides, hugging the bright-red car as he flashed forward at over eighty miles per hour. Shoppes, apartments, tall office buildings, and squat cafés flashed past on both sides, and then he rocketed around another much smaller roundabout.

He could see the tower now, rising out of the cityscape in majestic, semi-illuminated glory, with odd dark patches covering the middle section. Wolfgang slowed the Ferrari as he screeched into Jardins du Trocadéro. Directly ahead, the massive Trocadéro Garden's pool stretched out to either side, with a jet of water shooting out and arcing in graceful glory before falling into the pool halfway down its length. Soft lights illuminated the fountain and the surrounding green space, and directly to his left, the Eiffel Tower shot skyward, just on the other side of the river.

Wolfgang jerked the wheel to the left and slammed on the gas. He wasn't intimidated by the car anymore. He knew what it could do, and he knew he could handle it. He rocketed through the Gardens and then hit the bridge, laying on the horn to alert the handful of late-night pedestrians and lovers who leaned over the water under the light of the Eiffel Tower. They screamed and scattered as the Ferrari screeched across the river and then blew through the next intersection. Directly ahead, the tower's four legs spread out, surrounded by a low metal fence that blocked pedestrians from walking beneath it. Wolfgang hit the gas and burst through the fence at fifty miles an hour. Metal screeched down the sides of the car, and he cut the wheel to the right, spinning to a halt directly beneath Paris's most iconic monument.

Wolfgang threw the door open and rolled out as police sirens wailed in the distance. He tilted his head back and stared up into the interior of the tower, shielding his eyes. The tower was lit all along its frame, stretching up over one thousand feet into the Parisian sky. At odd intervals along the graceful metallic superstructure, tarpaulins blocked off the light, and scaffolding covered the tower. Stacks of barrels rose like a small mountain at the base of the tower, and the main tourist entrance was completely blocked off with yellow construction tape.

The tower was closed for maintenance. Wolfgang remembered reading about it in the travel brochure he picked up on the plane. Every seven years, the entire thing was repainted to preserve the metal from decay. The process took three years and consumed over sixty tons of iconic, bronze-colored paint.

The same paint that Spider's shoes were stained with.

Wolfgang scanned the base of the tower and immediately saw the elevator, the entrance of which was closed off with a metal gate. Faint footprints marked the concrete leading up to the elevator, with parallel tire marks running behind them. Small tires, like you might find on a hand truck. The gate swung open without resistance, but when Wolfgang reached for the keypad, nothing was there. The entire control panel had been smashed in and obliterated. There was no way to call the car.

Wolfgang felt the tension rising in his stomach, and he ran a hand through his hair.

Think. Think!

Spider must have smashed the control panel, which meant he had in fact been here. But there must be another way.

The stairs. The brochure said there were 674 steps between ground level and the second floor of the structure. 674 steps, at one step a second. That was eleven minutes. But there was no way he could travel that fast for that long.

Screw it.

It didn't matter. He had to go, now.

Wolfgang rushed to the nearest leg of the tower and tore aside the construction tape. He started running, clearing the first flight in seconds and turning up the next. Every step clapped beneath his feet as the expensive leather soles of his dress shoes smacked against the metal. He forced himself not to take more than one step at a time—it would be an easy win now that would cost him dearly in the long run.

Not even his daily six-mile runs, weight training, and swimming could have prepared him for the grueling reality of 674 steps as the brisk French wind tore through the open structure and blasted his face. That wind—something he may have enjoyed were it a romantic night under the stars with Megan—now filled him with dread. Spider would've counted on this wind, holding out, biding his time, waiting for the perfect French night when the wind was strong but there was no rain. Because that's how dirty bombs work. They explode with a blast only as strong as whatever ordinary explosives they're packed with—C4, or more likely, plain dynamite.

But the fallout . . . the fallout would be the real killer. Spider would've packed his bomb with pounds of radioactive waste—the kind of thing a man working in nuclear energy could have obtained—exhausted rods from the reactors that fueled power plants, cut into small pieces and packed inside a lead case around the explosives. That package would be so radioactive that even though Spider would've worn protective gear, some of it still would've saturated his skin. Enough to set off Wolfgang's watch when he searched Spider's lifeless body.

Then Spider would've taken that bomb to the top of the tower. It would be heavy, necessitating his use of the elevator. He wouldn't have stopped at the first floor, or even the second. He would've taken the bomb all the way to the top of the tower, almost one thousand feet in the air, where the wind was the strongest.

And that's where he'd set it off. High above a densely populated city, where the dynamite would blast outward in all directions, and the nuclear waste would be carried by the wind over thousands of city blocks, there to rain down on unsuspecting civilians and poison them with a certain death that would take days, if not weeks, to materialize.

It was enough to bring down the city. It was enough to break the French economy, which would topple the European Union's economy and then bring down the world economy. And that would bring chaos. Anarchy. Because Spider was an anarchist, and chaos is a hell of a weapon.

Wolfgang ran, pumping out one step at a time, panting, and not pausing for a second as he reached the first floor of the tower, 187 feet off the ground. He spun to the next set of stairs and ran.

He wasn't sure how many minutes had ticked by, but he knew the wind was growing stronger, blowing out of the west and ripping through the open superstructure of the tower. With every blast in his face, he imagined a sudden detonation high above him. He imagined the tower shuddering as metal blasted outward amid a ball of fire and a boom so loud it would shake the ground.

But then nothing. The noise would fade, and people would stand in shock and stare at the shattered top of their beautiful tower, unaware that death itself was in the wind, only seconds away.

Wolfgang leaned on the rail and heaved, his head spinning. He wasn't sure how much farther he had to go. He hadn't counted steps, but he knew he was at least halfway to the second floor. After that, there was only one way to the top—a final elevator.

Wolfgang pushed himself up the steps, refusing to stop. Megan was someplace in the city, unprotected, unaware. Lyle and Edric and Kevin would all certainly die if he didn't reach the top in time.

The steps blurred, and he heard the scream of police sirens far below. He glanced down to see blue lights flashing near the Ferrari, but he didn't care. He only cared about reaching the top in time.

Another hundred steps rocketed past in a blur. Wolfgang's legs burned, his chest heaved, and his head swam, but he kept going.

The second floor opened around him in a flash. Wolfgang skidded and slid, grabbing a railing and heaving. He looked around the observation deck and blinked in the blast of the wind as it ripped through the tower with a vengeance. Spider had picked a good night.

Wolfgang found the elevator to the top floor surrounded by the tattered remnants of torn construction tape. The control panel was also smashed, like the first elevator. But unlike the first, this panel was built directly into the thick steel of the tower framework, and while the buttons were busted, the housing was still intact. He pressed the top button, smacking and wiggling it a few times until a dim light lit up behind it. The doors rolled open, and Wolfgang lurched inside, then hit the button for the top floor. The doors closed as distant shouts drifted up from someplace farther down the tower. The police.

A dull whine rang from the motor, and the car

began moving up the final six hundred feet to the top. Wolfgang closed his eyes and forced himself to breathe evenly. The bomb could detonate at any moment, and if it did, he would certainly die. But if there were just five minutes left before the bomb went off . . .

The car rose, gaining speed. Wolfgang braced himself and suddenly wondered what he was going to do when he reached the top. He didn't know a *thing* about disabling a bomb. Did he cut the red wire or the blue?

The car ground to a halt, then the doors rolled open, and a fresh blast of wind ripped straight through Wolfgang's tux. Only a few feet ahead, the wall of the tower rose to waist-height, with a chain-link fence covering the space from the top of the wall to the tip of the tower. Observation scopes were mounted at intervals along the wall, and the observation deck encircled the top of the tower like a giant donut.

Wolfgang rushed outward, catching himself on the rail and staring straight below toward Paris. His stomach flipped, and he stumbled back, his knees feeling suddenly weak. He wasn't usually afraid of heights, but the vast distance between himself and the ground seemed cataclysmic. He imagined the bomb going off and him being hurtled off the tower and into the dead air beyond. Falling. Falling to his death.

Wolfgang shook his head and began to circle the observation deck, one corner, and then the second. The empty deck was smudged with half-dry paint and mucky footprints. Spider's footprints.

He grabbed the railing to steady himself, then turned the final corner. The bomb lay in the middle of the deck, planted like a forgotten suitcase. But it was much bigger than a suitcase—built into a 55-gallon drum, strapped to a hand truck with a lid pressed over the top.

Wolfgang rushed forward and pressed his fingers into the gap around the lid, then prized it up. The lid wouldn't move, and Wolfgang's fingers slipped off the rim with a pop.

He searched his pockets, but the only things he had left with him were his passport and a small bundle of Euros.

Think. Quickly.

Wolfgang felt around the side of the drum until his fingers found the ratchet of the strap binding it to the hand truck. A quick tug on the ratchet, and a press of the release switch, and the strap came loose. Wolfgang pulled it free of the drum and felt down its length until he found the metal hook tied to the strap's end. It was flat and stiff and fit perfectly into the gap around the drum's lip.

The lid was tightly battered down like the lid of a paint can, but as Wolfgang shoved down on the hook, he felt it give. Just a little at first, then more. A small gap opened at one side, and Wolfgang dropped the hook, shoving his fingers through the gap and jerking upward. The lid flew off, and the dim lights from the spire of the tower shone down inside the barrel.

Dynamite. It was packed in the middle of the barrel with unidentifiable metal cases crammed in all around it, each of them painted yellow with red radioactive labels on them. On top of the dynamite was a mess of multi-colored wires, a couple of circuit boards, and an LCD display counting down from six minutes.

How do I do this? Do I just rip away the wires?

No. Wolfgang had seen movies where people did that and the bomb ending up going off. Was this like the movies? Surely it wasn't that simple.

He wiped his face, and his hands shook. The clock read under five minutes now, ticking down one second at a time. With each flash of the screen, Wolfgang felt the wind at his back and imagined the top of the tower exploding into flames.

No. Think. Think!

Another flash caught his eye, and when he glanced down at the smartwatch on his arm, his heart lurched.

The watch. Lyle can see.

Wolfgang unlocked the watch and cycled through the apps but couldn't find a messenger or texting function. Had Lyle disabled it to make room for the other applications?

Come on . . . give me something!

Suddenly the watch's screen went black, and Wolfgang's stomach sank, thinking for a moment the battery had died. Then the screen flashed green and the whole watch lit up in single colors. Red. Yellow. Purple. The colors changed quickly, and Wolfgang felt the blood surge through him again. Lyle *could* see.

He directed the watch's camera to the top of the barrel as the screen went black again. Slowly, he maneuvered around the edge of the barrel, providing Lyle with different angles of the bomb.

The timer counted down under three minutes.

"Come on, Lyle!"

The screen flashed yellow. Wolfgang peered into the bomb case and dug through the wires until he located a yellow wire. He started to pull it, but then the watch began to flash through the different colors again.

"What?" he shouted. "I don't know what you want!"

The watch stopped flashing, and Wolfgang sucked in a breath. He closed his eyes and forced himself to think. He couldn't panic. Not now.

He opened his eyes and turned the watch until the camera faced him, then he slowly mouthed, "Two blinks . . . yes." He held up two fingers, then a thumbs-up. "Three blinks . . . no." Three fingers, then a thumbs-down. "Understand?"

The watched blinked blue, twice.

"All right, buddy. Let's get it done." Wolfgang leaned over the barrel and fingered the yellow wire. He held the watch to where Lyle could see, and then he waited.

The watch blinked red three times. Wolfgang dropped the wire and wiped his eyes, then dug through the barrel. The watch blinked yellow again, then black.

"That's the only yellow wire, Lyle!"

The clock on the bomb read one minute, twelve seconds. Wolfgang's heart thumped. The watch blinked yellow, then black. Yellow, then black. Wolfgang dug through the wires as the clock flashed rhythmically.

His fingers shuffled through a red wire, then a blue, and two green, then he touched a black wire. The watch flashed frantically: yellow, black, yellow, black.

Wolfgang twisted the wire and saw a yellow stripe running up its back side. He held the camera close to the wire. "This one?"

The watch flashed green, twice.

He snatched the wire, and it broke free of the mechanism, but the clock didn't stop ticking. Twenty seconds, now. Nineteen.

The watch flashed red. Wolfgang put his fingers on the red wire, and the watch flashed green, twice. Wolfgang snatched the wire.

Nine seconds. Eight seconds.

"Come on, Lyle!"

The watch flashed purple. Wolfgang dug frantically through the mess. Two purple wires ran into the same mechanism—neither with any stripes.

Four seconds. Three seconds.

He didn't have time to confirm with Lyle. He grabbed both wires and snatched them free of the mechanism.

The clock froze over the two-second mark, then went black. Wolfgang stumbled back until his hips hit the wall.

The bomb didn't go off.

He collapsed to the floor of the observation deck, nervous sweat streaming down his face despite the cold. He let out a soft sob and lowered his head into shaking hands.

I did it . . . I did it . . .

The elevator door rolled open on the other side of the tower, and footsteps rang against the deck. Two French police officers darted around the corner, guns drawn. They skidded to a halt only feet away, and Wolfgang leaned back against the wall, offering a tired smile.

"What's up, guys?"

The lead cop eyed the barrel, then his glare turned toward Wolfgang. He sniffed in indignant disgust and lifted a lip. "You are under arrest!"

Wolfgang grinned. "Sounds great, buddy."

[12]

French jail smelled just about the same as any institutional building in America—a cocktail of sweat, stale coffee, and too little ventilation, but Wolfgang didn't care. He lay on his cot, facing the ceiling with his eyes closed, and just breathed.

He was alive. In the heat of the moments leading up to disabling the bomb, he'd never thought about himself. He'd thought about his team, he'd thought about innocent Parisians, and he'd thought about Megan. It wasn't until the bomb was about to detonate that he really considered his own stake in the game, and even then the imminence of his death didn't sink in until the jailer locked the door and Wolfgang had a moment to think.

He wasn't worried about being in jail. Sure, he'd stolen a three-hundred-thousand-dollar car, scraped it up, broken several traffic laws, broken into a closed monument at night, and most auspiciously, been arrested next to a nuclear weapon. All those things would be cleared up by SPIRE, or they wouldn't. And if they weren't, if SPIRE disavowed him and left him in this cell . . . well, he was a man of many means. He'd get out eventually.

Right now he just wanted to lie on this bed, eyes closed, and enjoy being alive. The cot was stiff, and a stray spring jabbed into his back, but he didn't care. He could lie there for days, his eyes closed, a single image playing over and over in his mind—the image of him and Megan dancing at the gala, moving smoothly while the music played and the world around them faded out of existence.

He'd never met somebody so special that he thought about them this way or felt the things he was feeling now. He'd never met somebody that he thought he'd like to spend a lot of time with, and really get to know, and maybe even let her get to know him.

And yet, he knew it couldn't be. That was clear now. Sure, she'd only known him a few days, but she clearly didn't reciprocate the attraction he felt, and he thought he knew why.

Footsteps clicked against the concrete of the jail floor, and Wolfgang made a show of yawning without opening his eyes.

"Yo, Louis!" Wolfgang shouted. "When's breakfast? I feel like I'm entitled to some French toast."

"How about breakfast in the USA?" Megan stood just on the other side of the bars, leaned against them, staring at him with just the hint of a smile playing at her lips.

Wolfgang swung his feet onto the floor, breaking out into a grin as he walked toward her. "Finally! I thought you guys were gonna leave me here."

Megan shrugged. "That was certainly suggested, but you've got Lyle's watch. He wants it back."

Wolfgang laughed. "No way. They can bury me with that watch."

"Are you okay? Did they wash you off?"

Wolfgang nodded quickly, uneager to discuss the details of the French decontamination process. He appreciated being washed free of nuclear contaminants, but standing buck naked in somebody else's country while they sprayed you with a water hose . . . well. It wasn't a postcard moment.

More footsteps, and a cop appeared. It was the same cop who'd arrested him at the top of the tower.

The man's eyes were dark and full of disgust. He opened the door and held it back, sticking his nose in the air. "You are free to go."

Wolfgang grinned. "Don't mind if I do."

He and Megan walked back to the front desk, where he processed out. The paperwork he'd signed labeled him as Paul Listener, and he remembered the passport he'd taken to the gala.

They think I'm Canadian.

The desk clerk handed him the passport, along with the watch and euro notes. "You have twelve hours to leave France, Monsieur Listener."

Wolfgang flashed her his standby grin. "No worries. I'll be home by then."

He followed Megan outside and ducked into the waiting Mercedes. It was Kevin's car from earlier that night, but there was no sign of Kevin or the others. Sunlight streamed over Paris from the east, bathing the car in golden light and reminding Wolfgang how good it was to see another day.

"They're waiting on the plane," Megan said as she slipped into the driver's seat. "We'll take off as soon as we arrive."

"How did you get me out? I mean, they have to think I was at fault for the bomb."

Megan shrugged. "Edric made some calls. SPIRE pulled some strings. I imagine that if we stuck around another few hours, you'd be arrested again, but all we needed was an opening."

"Thanks," Wolfgang said.

He watched as Megan piloted the car onto the highway. Her hair was held back in a simple ponytail, and she wore a leather jacket and jeans. Somehow, she looked even better than she had in the dress.

He looked away, his stomach tightening. "How mad is Edric?"

"Edric is more flexible than he lets on. A lot happened last night. Were it not for you, a lot more would have happened."

"What about Spider? I found his body—"

"In the alley, yes. Edric already spoke to the CIA. Apparently Raven pushed too hard and blew his own cover. Spider wasn't talking, and Raven eliminated him, rather than letting him go."

"Sloppy work. I can't imagine the CIA is pleased."

"They're not," Megan said. "I get the feeling Raven will be out of a job pretty soon. How did you figure it out, anyway? Your comm went dead."

Wolfgang tapped the watch. "The Geiger counter went off in my watch when I searched Spider's body. It shouldn't have done that unless he'd been recently exposed to radiation. That's when I realized there must already be a bomb. A dirty bomb made the most sense. Constructing an actual nuclear device would require resources and know-how that even a nuclear scientist like Spider couldn't have obtained on his own. But a dirty bomb is just nuclear waste packed around an explosive. I figured Spider could've obtained the waste. So, then it was just a matter of where he put it."

"How the hell did you guess the Eiffel Tower?"

"There was paint on his shoes. I'd read that the

tower was being painted, and anyway, it made sense. Setting it off that high over the city would dramatically increase its effectiveness."

"Damn . . ." Megan shook her head, and Wolfgang thought he saw genuine respect in her eyes. "That was quick thinking," she said. "And quick driving."

Wolfgang laughed. "Yeah, too bad we can't take the Ferrari home. Hey, what about the Russians?"

"What about them?"

"Are they . . . alive?"

She nodded. "We ended up tasing the one outside. Your guy is gonna have one hell of a concussion, but he'll survive."

"I'm glad."

"You're glad?"

"He was never the enemy," Wolfgang said. "He was just doing his job."

Megan laughed. "Even so, I'd recommend you avoid dark alleys next time you're in Moscow."

"Hey, if it's up to me, I'll never *be* in Moscow."

The car grew quiet as they approached the airport. Megan rubbed her lip with one finger, glancing at him out of the corner of her eye. He didn't say anything, but he knew what she was thinking, and he was dreading the conversation.

"I know Kevin left his post," she said.

Wolfgang nodded. "Yep."

Megan put both hands on the wheel and let out a

breath. "There's . . . there's something you need to know about him. And me."

Wolfgang faced the window. "You're exes. I know."

"Exes?" Megan's voice turned shrill. "Gross! He's my brother."

"Your brother? What do you mean?"

"How many definitions does *brother* have?"

"You have different last names."

"Well, okay. Half brother. We share a mother."

"Wait, so . . ."

Megan held up a hand. "Just listen, okay?"

Wolfgang sat back and waited for Megan to clear her head. She stroked hair out of her face, and he thought he saw a tear forming in the corner of her eye.

"Edric told you we lost a man on our last mission."

Wolfgang nodded.

"His name was James. We worked together for a long time." Her voice wavered a little, but she regained control. "Kevin and James were best friends. They used to hang out a lot outside of work. Hunting trips and football games . . . James was more like a brother. They were very close."

Again, she paused, then swallowed, as if the next thing she had to say was going to be the hardest. "James and I were also . . . a thing. I mean, we were together. Dating, or whatever. Edric didn't know, or at least he pretended not to know, because of course it was a bad idea. The thing is, we worked so well together, I guess he figured it didn't matter if we were involved."

Wolfgang knew where this was headed, and he felt like a miserable, disgusting jerk.

"Our last mission was in Damascus. Edric, Kevin, and James were in a two-story building collecting intel from a terrorist organization. Something went wrong. The terrorists found them there, in the building."

Megan looked out her window, and for a long moment, she said nothing.

Wolfgang felt an overwhelming longing to grab her hand—to have her stop the car so he could hold her. But he waited.

Megan wiped her eyes and nodded a couple times. "Kevin blames himself for what happened. He was closest to James and Edric when the gunfire started. A hand grenade went off and blew Edric out of a second-floor window. He broke his shoulder and humerus on impact, but Kevin was able to get to him before the fighters closed in. James never made it out."

Megan nodded a couple times, as if she were accepting the reality of what had happened all over again. "It's my fault. I should have been there. They left me behind because, you know, it's Damascus. Women can't just go places without being noticed.

But maybe, if I'd been there . . ." She glanced at Wolfgang from the corner of her eye, as if remembering who she was talking to, then cleared her throat and sat up. "Anyway. I just thought you should know. I guess I was a little cold to you before. And Kevin came across a little ugly, I know. He's protective of me, and he feels like you're replacing James. He can't accept that."

Megan turned off the road and into the private airfield where the Gulfstream sat at the end of the runway, ready for takeoff. The others were already inside, and Wolfgang felt a strange comfort thinking about being around Edric and Lyle again. And Kevin.

"You won't have to worry about him now, anyway." Megan put the car in park. "Edric will fire him for leaving his post."

Wolfgang reached for the door handle, then felt Megan's hand on his. He flinched, lightning flooding his body, and when he turned, it surprised him to see her smiling.

She gave his hand a gentle squeeze. "I like you, Wolfgang. You're good at your job, and you're fun to have around. But you should know . . . I'll never become involved with somebody on my team again."

The exhilaration that flooded him only moments before crashed down like a house of cards. A weight descended into his stomach, and he nodded dumbly. Megan ducked out of the car, and he hurried to follow, feeling awkward and foolish as he ascended the steps into the plane.

The door shut automatically behind him, and he followed Megan into the cabin where Edric and Kevin were. Lyle sat in the back, hidden behind a computer screen.

Edric jumped up and hurried across the aisle, smacking Wolfgang on the back with his good arm. "Wolfgang! Dammit, it's good to see you. Hell of a job last night. Hell of a job!"

The warmth in Edric's tone was more than Wolfgang had ever heard him express. As the captain called for them to fasten their seatbelts, he took a seat across the aisle from Kevin, feeling the bigger man's eyes on him the entire time. As the seatbelt clicked, he glanced at Kevin and saw him look away.

There was a shadow in his eyes—a little shame, or a little sadness.

The plane's engines whined, then the aircraft shot down the runway, lifting into the air like a bird.

As soon as the seatbelt light went off, Wolfgang turned to Edric. "Hell of a thing with those Russians."

"What do you mean?"

Wolfgang shrugged. "If Kevin hadn't seen them walking in and come to warn me, they probably would've got the jump on us."

Edric's eyes narrowed, and Kevin sat up. They

both stared at Wolfgang. Lyle and Megan were watching him, also.

"He came to warn you?" Edric asked quietly.

Wolfgang nodded. "My earpiece was giving me trouble all night. Guess he couldn't get through. Right, Kev?"

Kevin's cheeks flushed, and he looked down. But he nodded. "Yeah . . . that's right."

Wolfgang could tell Edric wasn't fooled, but he said nothing. He stared at Wolfgang for a long moment, then grunted and slapped Kevin on the shoulder. "Good job, Kevin. Lyle, let's take a look at those earpieces."

Wolfgang walked to the tail of the plane, stopping at the minibar next to Lyle. He poured himself a water and sipped it, shooting Lyle a sideways glance.

The computer wiz smirked, then whispered, "There's nothing wrong with those earpieces if you charge them."

"Roll with me?" Wolfgang said.

"I guess I owe you one."

"Owe me one?"

Lyle's cheeks flushed red, and he turned back to the computer.

"Owe me for what?"

Lyle sniffed, and a grin tugged at his lips. "Oh, nothing. It's just that . . . the bomb was disabled after the second wire."

"What?"

Megan turned in her seat, and Wolfgang was suddenly aware that the entire plane was listening again.

He growled. "The *second* wire? What about the purple wire? You told me to pull the purple wire!"

"Sure," Lyle said. "That just disabled the clock."

Wolfgang slammed the glass down. "My god, man. I was about to have a heart attack!"

A ripple of laugher echoed through the plane, and Lyle broke into a grin. "Welcome to Charlie Team, Wolfgang."

WOLFGANG RETURNS IN...

Turn the page to read the first chapter for free.

THAT TIME IN CAIRO
BOOK 2 OF THE WOLFGANG PIERCE SERIES

September, 2011

Even in late summer, Buffalo was cool. Sharp wind drifted off Lake Erie and tore through the city like the revenging hand of God, searching for anybody who may be guilty of being comfortable. Only weeks from now, the snow would start, and a month after that, it would clog Buffalo, piled high against every building. For now, standing outside was still bearable, but the shortening days and sharpening wind were an omen of what lay ahead.

Wolfgang stood thirty yards from the building with his hands jammed into the pockets of a light windbreaker. From his vantage point on the sidewalk, he could see through the smeared windows and into the dingy interior of Jordan Fletcher Home for Children. Harried workers ran back and forth, dressed in scrubs featuring safari animals, while children played in any number of small rooms with colorful walls.

These were the outcasts—the orphans and the lonely—children who were between foster homes or awaiting an impending adoption mired in red tape. Wolfgang knew their stories because he was one of them, and so was Collins.

Through the third story of the shabby building, Wolfgang could see her room. It was small, with a mechanical bed lifted into a seat. Collins's room was more akin to a hospital room than a child's bedroom. Sure, the same bright paints adorned the walls, and the same toys littered the floor, but Collins didn't run and play like the other children. She didn't laugh as loud or walk as fast.

And she never would.

Wolfgang found a park bench that faced the facility. The wooden slats of the bench creaked under his weight, but it felt good to sit. He watched the little room on the third floor. From this angle, he could just make out the top of the bed and the small, curly-haired head that rested against a pillow. Eyes shut. Cheeks pale.

Another blast of lake wind tore down the street, crashing around Wolfgang's windbreaker like water over rock, but he didn't move. He didn't even shudder. Wolfgang just watched the room, thinking of Collins, and for the dozenth time that year, he told himself to get up and go inside. Go to her room . . . sweep her up in a hug. Tell his baby sister that he loved her.

But he couldn't.

He closed his eyes and heard the crash of glass against hardwood. He heard the yell of a drunken man out for blood. The scream of a panicked woman shielding her children. The broken sob of a little girl, her breaths ragged and filled with pain.

"Throw that runt out!" the man had screamed. "No child of mine is defective!"

More glass shattered. More household items flew like artillery shells, exploding against marred drywall, already battered by a hundred such engagements.

And so it went, two, sometimes three nights a week—as often as the man found the bottle, and the bottle found the floor, and the little girl cried and sheltered behind her bruised mother while her older brother cowered in the shadows . . . and did nothing.

Wolfgang opened his eyes. They stung with cold tears as the wind intensified. He couldn't see Collins's head now, but he imagined he could. He imagined he could hear her breaths, each one filled with pain as the ravages of her disease clutched her body.

He stood up, leaning into the wind and hurrying across the street, then stopped in front of the smudged glass entrance and stared at the handle.

Wolfgang turned to the right and approached the donation slot next to the door. He dug a thick envelope from beneath the windbreaker, packed with anonymous cash, and crammed it through the slot. Casting another furtive glance at the window, three floors up, he whispered to Collins as he always did. "I love you, and one day, I'll make it right."

Wolfgang's phone buzzed. He turned from the building and retrieved it, grateful for the distraction. There was a text message from a contact labeled simply as E.

HEADQUARTERS. 12 HOURS.

A flood of excitement filled him—enough to burn away the cold, but never quite enough to burn away the guilt. He shoved the phone back into his pocket and held out his hand for the nearest taxi.

Buffalo might've been in the throes of premature fall, but in St. Louis, summer was still alive and well. Wolfgang found Charlie Team waiting for him on the fourteenth floor of the Bank of America Plaza, and he scrubbed his shoes on the mat outside the door before ducking inside.

"Wolfgang! Better late than never," Edric called from the far side of the room.

Wolfgang blushed, glancing around the room to see Lyle sitting behind a computer at the table and

Kevin standing next to the minibar, mixing a cocktail. Megan sat by herself next to the window, right where she had the first time he'd met her four months prior. She leaned against the wall with her legs crossed and stared out at the gleaming Gateway Arch only a half mile away. She wore yoga pants and a loose-fitting shirt that fell an inch short of her waistline. She was beautiful in a simple, elegant way. He loved that.

"Like a drink, Wolf?" Kevin's commanding voice boomed from the minibar, and the big man offered Wolfgang a reserved nod.

"A Sprite would be great," Wolfgang said.

Kevin reached for the soda as Wolfgang settled into a chair. This was Charlie Team—an elite detachment of SPIRE, a company specializing in professional espionage services. They worked for whoever could pay their hefty fees, conducting specialized undercover missions around the globe. Their diverse capabilities were prominently advertised in their name: Sabotage, Procurement, Infiltration, Retaliation, and Entrapment. SPIRE did it all.

Wolfgang joined Charlie Team earlier that summer after working for SPIRE as an independent operator for three years, conducting corporate espionage and entrapment rackets in mostly American cities. Now his missions would carry him around the globe. In June, the team had barely survived a delicate operation in Paris, which almost cost a great deal more than their own lives. Wolfgang thrived on that mission, winning the respect of the rest of the team, but failing to win everything he really wanted.

As Megan sat next to the window, he heard her words play back from moments before they left Paris. *"I like you, Wolfgang. But you should know . . . I'll never become involved with somebody on my team again."*

Wolfgang looked away, shoving his feelings deep inside a mental box and locking them there. Megan was right, after all. They were a team. They had a job to do. Getting involved with each other didn't play a part in that.

"Here you go." Kevin offered Wolfgang the Sprite with another reserved nod.

Kevin was Megan's half brother, and prior to the Paris mission, he was about as friendly with Wolfgang as a dog with a burglar. Wolfgang could still feel the awkward tension between them, fueled predominantly by Kevin's suspicions that Wolfgang was making a play for his sister, but at least Kevin was handing him drinks now instead of throwing punches. Wolfgang could appreciate the progress.

"Thanks, Kev."

Wolfgang sipped the soda as Edric approached his favored whiteboard and produced a red marker. Edric's right arm moved with a little stiffness—residual effects of a multi-point break from an accident in Damascus five months prior. The injury had hamstrung Edric in Paris, and Wolfgang wondered how much it would limit them on whatever mission lay ahead.

"I hope you guys had a nice break. We're back at it, and we're going someplace warm."

Edric started scratching on the board, and Wolfgang wondered why he bothered. It seemed needlessly time-consuming and repetitious.

"Cairo," Edric said, stepping back. "We're going to Cairo."

Edric grinned at the room as if he were awaiting a standing ovation, but Cairo wasn't exactly the warm, exotic locale Wolfgang had imagined. Nassau or Fiji would've hit the spot. Havana, even. Cairo?

Edric sighed, then turned to the board and drew a large triangle. "Cairo," he said. "Great Pyramids?"

Lyle started slow-clapping, and the others quickly joined in. Edric rolled his eyes and motioned to the table. "You're all jerks. Gather up."

Megan, Kevin, and Wolfgang joined Lyle at the table.

"Three weeks ago," Edric said, "a construction worker laboring on an apartment building in the Libyan village of Al Jawf uncovered a stone case that housed an ancient papyrus scroll inscribed with hieroglyphics. It seems he didn't really know what he'd found, but he thought it might be valuable, so he went into town and found an American W.H.O. worker and tried to sell it. The American had enough education to recognize the extreme age of the scroll and bought it from him, then called Libyan authorities."

Edric wrote on the board the entire time he spoke, sketching words such as *scroll* and *W.H.O.* and connecting them with a mess of lines that, at first glance, made the entire story appear to be the structure of an elaborate bank heist.

"The Libyans deployed some researchers to take a look, and they determined the scroll to date back to around one thousand B.C., possibly a relic of the Library of Alexandria. Obviously a valuable find."

"Why do I detect the sordid stench of impending corruption?" Kevin asked.

Edric just smirked. "The Libyans confiscated the scroll from the W.H.O. worker and contacted Egyptian authorities. Apparently, Libya hasn't got much interest in ancient literature, but they thought they could make a quick buck. After some haggling, Egypt agreed to purchase the scroll. They sent scientists to authenticate it, then placed it in a protective, vacuum-sealed case . . ."

"And lost it," Megan finished.

Edric jabbed the marker at her. "Bingo. Someplace between Al Jawf and Cairo—amid a thousand kilometers of Sahara desert—the case went missing, along with its escorts."

"They drove straight through the desert?" Megan asked.

"Yep. The research team from Cairo hasn't been

seen or heard from in six days, but one of the Land Rovers used in the convoy turned up in southern Egypt earlier this week, riddled with bullet holes."

"Shit," Kevin muttered.

"What's the value of the scroll?" Wolfgang asked.

Edric shrugged. "The Egyptians bought it for one hundred twelve thousand Libyan dinars. About twenty-five thousand dollars, US."

"Not a lot to kill for," Wolfgang said.

"No, not really," Edric said. "Except the Egyptians believe the scroll was worth more than ancient porn. Almost none of it was readable without restoration, but what snippets they gathered indicate the document to be some kind of burial record. The map to a tomb, if you will."

Silence filled the room as the morbid quality of the words sank in.

Edric nodded slowly, then sat down at the end of the table. "At least a dozen tombs of the pharaohs have yet to be found," he said. "When King Tut's tomb was discovered in 1922, they valued the contents at tens of millions."

Wolfgang let out a low whistle. "Plenty to kill for."

Edric nodded. "Grave robberies have accounted for the destruction of numerous ancient artifacts and national treasures in Egypt. The Egyptian government wants to be sure that whatever tomb is documented on the scroll isn't the next victim."

"So, they hired us to catch a book thief?" Kevin laughed.

"You could say that," Edric said. "Only, this book thief is well armed, probably not alone, and lost in the biggest desert on the planet."

Wolfgang fingered the dripping condensation on the outside of the Sprite can, evaluating the story and searching for inconsistencies or missing information. Then he grinned. "Well, *procurement* is in our name, right? Let's go procure a grave map."

READY FOR MORE?

Visit LoganRyles.com for details.

ABOUT THE AUTHOR

Logan Ryles is the author of the multiple page-turning thrillers featuring fan favorite character Reed Montgomery. You can learn more about Logan's books, sign up for email updates, and connect with him directly by visiting LoganRyles.com.

ALSO BY LOGAN RYLES

THE WOLFGANG PIERCE SERIES

Prequel: *That Time in Appalachia* (read for free at LoganRyles.com)

Book 1: *That Time in Paris*

Book 2: *That Time in Cairo*

Book 3: *That Time in Moscow*

Book 4: *That Time in Rio*

Book 5: *That Time in Tokyo*

Book 6: *That Time in Sydney*

THE REED MONTGOMERY SERIES

Prequel: *Sandbox*, a short story (read for free at LoganRyles.com)

Book 1: *Overwatch*

Book 2: *Hunt to Kill*

Book 3: *Total War*

Book 4: *Smoke and Mirrors*

Book 5: *Survivor*

Book 6: *Death Cycle*

Book 7: *Sundown*

THE PROSECUTION FORCE SERIES

Book 1: *Brink of War*
Book 2: *First Strike*
Book 3: *Election Day*

LoganRyles.com

Made in the USA
Monee, IL
12 August 2022